MY FAVOURITE

SARAH JOLLIEN-FARDEL

Translated by

HOLLY JAMES

THE
INDIGO
PRESS

THE INDIGO PRESS
50 Albemarle Street
London W1S 4BD
www.theindigopress.com

The Indigo Press Publishing Limited Reg. No. 10995574
Registered Office: Wellesley House, Duke of Wellington Avenue
Royal Arsenal, London SE18 6SS

First published in Great Britain in 2024 by The Indigo Press
First published in France in 2022

A CIP catalogue record for this book is available from the British Library

ISBN: 978 1 911648703
eBook ISBN: 978 1 911648697

This book has been selected to receive financial assistance from English PEN's PEN Translates programme, supported by Arts Council England. English PEN exists to promote literature and our understanding of it, to uphold writers' freedoms around the world, to campaign against the persecution and imprisonment of writers for stating their views, and to promote the friendly co-operation of writers and the free exchange of ideas.

www.englishpen.org

Cover design © Luke Bird
Cover image © doit / iStock
Art direction by House of Thought
Author photo © Marie-Pierre Cravedi
Typeset by Tetragon, London
Printed and bound in Great Britain by TJ Books Limited, Padstow

Supported using public funding by
ARTS COUNCIL
ENGLAND

For my grandmother Sylvie

Who has not found the Heaven – below –
Will fail of it above –
For Angels rent the House next ours,
Wherever we remove –

Emily Dickinson, 'Poem 1544'

I

All of a sudden, he has a gun in his hands. One minute ago, I swear, we were eating potatoes. Practically in silence. My sister, though, was chattering away as usual. My father would say: 'She can't keep her trap shut, that one.' But she kept babbling on. She was naive, joyful, a bit silly. Funny and kind. She wasn't the sharpest at school. She wouldn't notice changes in my father's breathing, the look in his eye that meant we were in for a good hiding. She never stopped talking. I, on the other hand, was constantly on my guard, never able to relax. Fear always clung to my body. I saw my mother's frailty. My father's cruelty, his stupidity. I saw my big sister's innocence. I saw everything. I knew I wasn't cut from the same cloth as them. My weakness was my pride. It gave me courage and kept me going. I was a child. I understood things without knowing.

The scenario was always the same. He'd come home after a day on the road, reeking of alcohol. If he sat down on the decrepit leather sofa in the living room and fell asleep, the three of us knew we'd have a few hours' peace. If he sat his enormous body on a chair in the kitchen and grabbed a knife to crack open some nuts or slice a piece of one of the cheeses he'd been leaving to mature in the earthen cellar, we were in for it. That's how terribly banal it was. The same old scene playing out repeatedly, with each of us in our preordained roles. None of us could see things from an audience's perspective. All four of us were dancing the same waltz, following the steps in the choreography. None of us had the sense or indiscretion to put a foot out of line.

It could be a stringy piece of meat in the stew. It could be a superfluous clove, a chewy bay leaf, an overcooked carrot, a chunk of onion. It could be the rain, or the stifling heat in the cab of his lorry. It could be nothing at all. And so it would begin. The screaming, the fear, those awful words, a glass smashing against a wall, a slap around my mother's face or my sister's. And me, scurrying beneath the table, moving in time to that all-too-familiar family dance. Sometimes I'd see my mother fall down in front of me and curl up in a ball on the floor. Her eyes would scream in fear, her eyes would scream *Run!* and I'd bolt, hiding under the bed. Watching, observing. Deciding. Stay or make a run for it? But not once did I ever cover my ears. My sister would clap her hands firmly over hers. I wanted to hear. I had to listen out for clues, to know whether he'd gone too far this time. I had to listen to the words, every single one: dirty whore, slut, you were nobody before I met you, look at the state of you, stupid bitch, I'm going to kill you. Behind the words, hate, misery, shame. And fear. The words were important. I had to listen to every one of them. The intonation. From watching it all happen, I was able to tell whether he was too drunk or too tired to go all the way, whether it would come to blows. Whether he was going to exhaust himself or whether he had enough strength to push my mother against a wall or a table and hit her.

Sometimes I heard his voice, all sweetness and light. That was the worst. I didn't understand how or why my mother and sister could be lulled by his saccharine tones. How they didn't see that it was a prelude to his hatred. They always believed – and above all hoped – that this time it would be different. Perhaps it was worse for me, knowing. I felt like his accomplice. When I saw it coming, I'd make up an excuse about having homework so I could get away. Or I'd clear the table as quickly as possible so there wouldn't be anything to hand that he could throw in our faces. Bottles were the worst. He'd hurl them against the walls, and we'd have to duck to avoid them as they went catapulting through the air. I was afraid of the heavy enamel jug my mother used for juice. Once, I managed to steal a plastic one from a department store when she and I were out shopping. My mother had a scar along her hairline close to her temple, where she'd been hit by a shard of glass from one of those cursed bottles. 'A bad fall,' she had told the doctor. I thought her hair was magnificent. Thick and straight. Nothing like mine. I loved to snuggle up to her and stroke it while she was knitting or reading, twisting her caramel locks around my index finger. My own hair was dark, drab and poker straight. It didn't have any natural highlights. It was dull and perpetually tangled. Sometimes I'd press my nose up to her hair, close my eyes and breathe in the scent. Timidly, she always told me to stop. The idea that I might find her beautiful embarrassed her.

At the shopping centre, I tried to come up with little schemes to get her to buy the ninety-nine-franc plastic jug that wouldn't hurt if he threw it at us. It was too expensive, and he kept track of every franc we spent. She said no. Two days later, when she sent me off to buy butter and polenta, I managed to steal the jug and stash it in my school backpack. I was sweating, my heart in my throat, but I did it. I set it down on the scratched wooden table (which had also been a victim of my father's violence), stood tall and looked her in the eye.

'Where did you get the money for that?' she asked.

I'd worked out a ploy. I'd stopped on the way home, rubbed dirt onto the jug, scratched it with a small pebble and rinsed it in the village pond. 'Sophie's mum wanted to throw it out. I told her I needed a jug for painting, so she gave it to me.'

When you tell a lie, there's that moment where time is suspended, a fraction of a second where everything hangs in the balance. I knew how to hold her gaze. I never looked away. I knew how to play innocent. Eyes wide, I twisted my lips into a thin, fake smile. It worked without fail.

My mother and sister were so alike, both physically and in terms of their reactions, that over time it made me think: If I wasn't like them, I must be like him. How else could I explain the fact that he'd look away whenever I stared at him? That although he'd pull my hair, he never once hit me? He never beat me, never grabbed me by the shoulders the way he did with them, shaking them like plum trees. Except once.

I was sitting at the kitchen table. It was a Sunday evening. He'd gone out, as he did every Sunday after lunch. We never knew what he did with his Sunday afternoons. I was curious about those hours he spent away from home. I wanted to know where he went, who he was with. Whenever I asked my mother, she would dodge the question by saying something trite or asking a question of her own, like 'What's wrong with the three of us just spending time together?' I wanted to escape him, yet everything continued to revolve around him. He had the presence of a terrorist, the power to change the atmosphere of any setting. I had no choice but to obsess about him constantly. My mother was cooking a coujenaze, a humble home recipe made with potatoes and beans, cooked on a low flame until the water completely evaporates. The flavours all marry without the ingredients tuning to mush. The beans are tender, the potatoes melt in the mouth. My mother could cook something out of nothing. Because she had nothing. She had to scrimp and save where she could. She wouldn't even dream of touching the small change she'd fish out of my father's trouser pockets before putting a wash on. With him, nothing was free. He once hit her for taking five centimes he'd deliberately left out on the table to test her. She'd scrape chicken off the bones and save them to make stock with. She would often have to ask the owner of the little shop in our village for things on credit. My father bought a pig each year. 'A pig for my sows,' he would say.

That Sunday, as twilight fell, I was drawing a picture of a tiger in our kitchen. He was a friendly tiger; he didn't look dangerous at all. He had a stripy little face and was wearing a red-and-yellow cap with a blue jumper. I folded the sheets of paper in half, then stapled along the fold. The little book, which I'd cobbled together in all my childish clumsiness, contained a story I'd made up. I don't remember now what it was about. All I remember is the feeling of excitement that came with putting one word after another to create something. It wasn't complicated. But it transported me far away from the house. I'd relished those hours lying on my stomach on my bed, watching the sentences form all by themselves until the final full stop. Whenever I think about it, I get that same intense rush of emotion. Taking those well-known words and arranging them in my own way, choosing one adjective over another, creating something that wouldn't exist if it weren't for me. It wasn't a question of pride. It was a solitary pleasure that had the immense magical power to take me away from my life.

He looked over my shoulder as I was putting the finishing touches to my feline friend. I was no good at drawing, but I still needed a cover for my book. I don't know what moved him that day. The carefree innocence of me concentrating on my colouring, arm at a right angle, or the smell of the meal, or the homely environment, the idealized picture of a family that greeted him as he walked into the kitchen and saw us there, my mother and me.

Perhaps it had to do with whatever he'd been up to that afternoon. All I know is that when he placed his large, calloused hand on my head, I immediately stiffened, defensive.

'What are you up to?'

'What does it look like?'

'Don't get smart with me.' He pulled his hand away.

I knew better than to provoke him, but this was the one pleasure he wasn't going to spoil: the profound joy I got from perfecting my little story, the prospect of showing my teacher the following day. In the boldest, haughtiest tone I could muster at the grand age of eight, I replied: 'That, my dear friend, is a tiger.'

2

My *dear friend*. As we were leaving Mass, I'd heard those words, spoken by Dr Fauchère, whom we deferentially referred to as 'The Doctor'. The Doctor was one of the few people in our village back then who had a degree. That morning, Gaudin the butcher had given the Doctor a little bow on the church esplanade. Dr Fauchère interrupted his conversation to say: 'Morning, my dear friend.' How elegant those words sounded coming from his mouth. That warm smile, just the right amount of politeness and restraint. I saw how that 'my dear friend' gave the speaker an air of importance and made it clear to their interlocutor that they were not of the same rank. In a gentle, subtle way. So I decided to be bold and say it myself: 'My dear friend.' My father was not an educated man, but he had that instinct bad people and animals have. Like Micky, my sister Emma's cat, who knew never to get under my father's feet and would scurry away as soon as his sky-blue Peugeot 404 pulled up to the house. Before then, I'd never let my silent hatred and contempt show. But that one phrase was the first shot in a battle that not even death could bring an end to.

I could have seen it coming. I had my senses constantly set to high alert, and fear as my compass. The second I said it, he grabbed me by the head and lifted me up. The chair fell backwards. My ears were locked in his ogre-like grip. I saw my mother standing in front of me, petrified. He let go, I fell to the floor. I thought it was over. Just another fit of temper. Then he dragged me by the forearm from the kitchen to my bedroom, my whole body banging against doors and walls as I went. I heard my mother screaming his name. I think that was the first time I'd ever heard her say it. 'Louis, no! Louis! Leave her alone, she's only little.' Louis closed the bedroom door. I didn't have time to get up. There was a pain radiating from my shoulder. I was on the floor, and he hit me on the behind and on the back. He turned me over and clamped his hands tightly around my neck. His face was deformed, eyes bulging and demented. And he was smiling. It was awful. The sight of it, the sensations in my body. Never before had I experienced the way a person's features can be transformed by pleasure, by having power over someone, but that night I witnessed the effect of that bestial force. On a man. A father. Mine. Standing over me, he loosened the grip of his giant hands and started swinging for my skinny body. First my head, then my chest, my arms. I didn't try to protect myself. I stared at him, stunned, eyes so wide my eyelids were hurting.

My mother swung a frying pan at his head, bald but for a few hairs. He stopped dead in shock. He got up and sent her flying against the wall with an almighty smack. I was shaking. I had wet myself without realizing it. I didn't cry; I threw up, I passed out.

I remember the hushed voices, the warm caress of a cloth on my forehead, the dim light. When I half-opened my eyes, there was my mother, and behind her Dr Fauchère. The Doctor. Our saviour. He was going to pull us out of that stinking hole. I knew it. He had gentle eyes. He wasn't like the others. I could tell he was educated, and his intelligence, I thought, would be our salvation.

'Been playing the stuntman, have you, Jeanne?'

He was teasing me, he had to be. What's worse? A clueless old bastard or a discerning man who's so cowardly he looks the other way when an eight-year-old girl gets beaten to a pulp? At that point, I hadn't yet grown to despise him. Perhaps I just needed to tell him straight. Perhaps I didn't look as bashed-up as I felt. 'It was my dad.'

'Your daddy? You want to see your daddy? He's not here.'

'No, no, no…' It was a prayer. *No, no, no.* I tried to shout it, but my voice was too thin. 'No. My dad. He hit me.'

The Doctor touched my forehead. 'It'll pass. Keep an eye over her overnight.' More hushed voices: I was being betrayed by the man I had still revered that very morning. I'd observed his facial expressions at the clinic, at Sunday Mass. I'd created a character for him, a figure of benevolence, kind and superior. I'd been blind to the hypocrisy, the self-importance. He'd repeatedly demonstrated – with a knowing smile, a glance, a frown, a tilt of the head – his sophistication and superiority to the rest of the oafs in our village. And, being the proud child I was, I was quick to mimic good old Dr Fauchère. My mimicry had earned me an almighty beating, a dislocated shoulder, bruises, a body that ached all over. Those stolen words proved that everyone had their place: the simpletons belonged to one rank, the bourgeoisie to another. And us simpletons, with our tiny, insignificant lives, were not permitted to use that kind of language. That little pat on my head shattered the last remaining illusions I had.

Dr Fauchère left the village shortly after that dismal episode. Years later, I would be hospitalized in Lausanne with viral meningitis. I don't know whether the Doctor saw my surname on the register, whether it stirred up emotional memories of home or repressed guilt. Either way, the nurse made the indiscreet remark that 'the Doctor' had been asking after me personally. She seemed impressed. I certainly wasn't. Of course not. It doesn't do for a man to spend his life with a definite article in front of his name. The headache lasted for days. A horrible ordeal. As I lay there, cooped up in the darkness, motionless as a corpse, even a tear escaping from the corner of my eye felt like torture.

By the time he paid me a visit, I was over the worst of it. In a deft movement, arms outstretched like the Messiah, my dear friend the Doctor entered my room. He looked delighted to see me. He launched into the typical niceties of small-town folks reunited in the big city, and the hatred I'd been holding back since that Sunday twenty years ago immediately flared up in every pore, every atom, every ounce of my flesh. I wanted to scream, blow a fuse, take the feelings that had been festering all this time and unleash them on the spineless doctor.

I remained rigid, paralysed by my own obstinacy and contempt. I kept the rage contorting my stomach locked away and fixed him with a steely gaze. He may have been the Doctor, an esteemed man back in the village, he may have been head of a university hospital, but evidently he hadn't been able to forget the cowardice I hadn't been able to forgive. The only thing worse than the mistakes seen by others are those we keep to ourselves, the ones that eat away at our souls. In our silent confrontation that day, my contemptuous look told him precisely what I thought of him.

I turned away from him, a slightly theatrical gesture. 'Coward.'

He heard it just before the door closed. I watched his head retract into his shoulders.

I wasn't yet thirty and already I was at war. I've always been at war. I always will be.

3

My father had a stranglehold on our home. Luckily, he was often away. During those days of respite, we lived almost like a normal family. My mother, Claire, was an avid reader of romance novels. When we took the bus into the city, one Wednesday afternoon per month, we would always go to the bookshop. Without fail. For a few francs, we would leave with a pile of dusty, battered books that would keep us enraptured for a few weeks. Luckily, my father hadn't the slightest clue about the infinite pleasure we got from this blissful form of escape. Otherwise, he would have forbidden it. It was a women's thing to him. A harmless little hobby. Ever on the alert, even when lost in our books we made sure he never got wind of this secret indulgence. Whenever he wasn't around, Mum would take immense pleasure in reading her romance novels in the green velvet armchair by the lace-curtained windows while I sat at her feet or in my bedroom. Emma, who hated reading, would be roaming around outside, playing with her cat or chasing the two red hens we used to have. My mother's family had disowned her after she fell pregnant with my sister. She had disgraced them by having sex before marriage. She married my father in a shotgun wedding, with two witnesses as their only guests. Every now and then, I'd look up from the book I was reading – *The Adventures of Fantômette*, or later, when my mother allowed me, one of her favourite authors, Guy des Cars – and press her for answers.

'Why did you marry him?'

'I felt sorry for him. He had just lost his mother.'

'Did you love him?'

'I pitied him. I made a mistake and I had to take responsibility. That's all there is to it.'

'But in the books they say love is a beautiful thing. *You* even say it. You say the stories in the books are beautiful.'

'That's enough now, Jeanne. They're just stories.'

I never learned more about their dismal, shambolic relationship, or how it came to be.

In mountain villages back in those days, divisions between social classes weren't as clear-cut, because they weren't marked by all the pageantry. Being rich simply meant owning land or, the peak of success, working in the public sector. To us, civil servants were important people. The rest of us were the children of labourers, craftsmen or farmers. My father, a lorry driver, earned a decent salary, which should have been enough to keep us out of poverty. But money wasn't the source of our impoverishment. Instead, it came from my father's violent acts, his ignorance, the verbal abuse and closed-mindedness. As I got older and my school days were nearly over, my father would often make a point of stating, out of nowhere, that we did not belong to the upper class: 'You'll go and get a job, just like your sister.' He decreed that I would work as a waitress or in the city watch factory, like people did in his day. My mother tried in vain to reason with him. She eventually conceded defeat, unable to stand up to his threats. Not me.

My teacher, Madame B, was firm but fair. And I had a strong and very personal sense of justice. Madame B was impartial. She once smacked her own niece, who had dared to act up, thinking herself exempt from punishment thanks to her family ties. I sensed the fire in Madame B's belly. I had experienced the injustice of violence first-hand, but Catherine deserved what she got. I caught Madame B's frightened gaze at the sight of blood flowing from her niece's nose. She was wearing a hefty signet ring that had rendered the action more forceful than intended. For a fraction of a second, I could tell she was shocked, then she pulled herself together, masking her distress. That's when I knew I had an accomplice on hand. She would help me fulfil my stubborn desire to continue my studies. She wouldn't let up.

I walked along the corridor. There were only three classrooms on each floor of the local school. I handed Madame B my registration form for a five-year course at teaching college. I had already passed the entrance exam. She gave me a warm smile. 'You want to be a schoolteacher, do you?'

'I don't know if I'll be a teacher or carry on studying to become a lecturer.'

She nodded tenderly. She was probably aware of the situation at home. The whole village was teeming with spiteful gossips. She looked at the form. The parent signature was missing. I knew what I was getting her into by handing her the form with that one box blank. I needed her to plead my case to my father. I didn't have to ask twice. She seemed unfazed. 'Leave it to me. I'll talk to your mother.' *Your mother*. I ticked the box marked 'boarding'. I had no idea how they managed it. But when September came around, I started the five-year course.

Those years felt like purgatory. A period of respite that was neither peaceful nor particularly eventful after the fifteen-year reign of terror that bled its way into every aspect of my daily life. I was petrified by the slightest noise – a draught slamming a door would make my breath catch in my chest; my room-mates rummaging through the dresser in the morning would send me straight back to those nights when my father, getting ready to leave for his shift, would rip out the drawers because he couldn't find a sock or a jumper, screaming at my mother: 'You lazy bitch! You don't do anything! You can't even do the washing for your husband, who's slaving away for you like a fucking idiot.'

It would take me a decade to be able to stop walking with a stoop, ducking every time I heard the creaking of furniture or footsteps on floorboards. But a lifetime wouldn't be enough to cure my aching, upset stomach. I was withdrawn, but I would occasionally speak out valiantly against injustices on the teaching course (whether real or imagined), which earned me a certain respect from my classmates, even though my scowl and knitted brow didn't do much for my popularity.

Back then, it was still a girls' school. Those young girls introduced me to the indecipherable and incomprehensible codes of seduction and the vital importance of this or that brand of clothing. I had never tried to make myself attractive, let alone considered the prospect of seduction. I had never experienced feelings of love or desire, other than the desire to escape my father. I never connected with anyone. How could I tell them I had more important things to think about than the various colours of Burlington socks? I never stood up to those who gave the 'less advanced' girls a hard time. That's what they called the girls who were still full of childlike innocence. Selfishly, I was glad, because it meant I got a break during those years. A period of convalescence. But it was at that age, when I lost what little innocence I had left, that I became callous. That was my way of surviving, of protecting myself from the damage I had fled but which continued to torment me. The first few times I returned home were painful. My mother tried to hide her sadness; I pretended not to see her bruises. In the end I somehow managed to make an arrangement with the nuns at my school so I wouldn't have to go home at weekends. Even if people were aware of abuse going on, nobody asked any questions. Like a coward, I left my mother alone with him, just as all my teachers had left us alone with him. Despite my selfishness, the rejection, absence and escapes, my mother was never anything but happy for me. Not once was I met with reproach or judgement. Only her kind smile.

There was never any reading between the lines, hidden meanings, no *Why don't we ever hear from you.* We'd occasionally meet by the post office or in front of the boarding school. We'd have to make it quick, as my father timed her outings to the minute.

As for my sister, I'd meet her in town. She was four years older than me, and although physical appearance had been nothing more than an abstract concept within the family home, her beauty revealed itself outside. I hadn't seen it clearly myself before, but I noticed how men behaved as she bent over to pour a glass of Goron for the regulars at the bar where she worked. Like I said, she wasn't the sharpest. But she was good with people. She'd laugh at their jokes, entertain them with her offhand comments, catch their attention with a swish of the hips. Old men, timid girls, temperamental children, surly women: everyone was captivated by her. She was seductive, and it was too much. She was provocative, a tease. I felt uncomfortable seeing her breasts sticking out beneath her shirts or dresses, which were always a little too low-cut. I loved her for the simple fact that she was my sister, and I'd often visit her at work. She'd always be drinking, cooing away. She'd kiss me on the cheek, I'd leave. I could never get enough of her comforting presence, even if it seemed like I was indifferent to her.

She was living above the bistro on Rue de Conthey, in a studio flat that belonged to one of her bosses. It was only later that I realized what she was doing there, why the customers were so nice to her. I often tried to talk to her about our father, but she'd dance around the issue, make a joke or give a deep sigh, saying: 'Let it go, Jeanne, that's just the way it is.'

Not long after the wine harvest celebrations in late September, as I was going into my second year, my sister invited me over for dinner. I made my way up the crooked stairs to her studio beneath the rooftops of one of the typically cramped buildings in the old town. I was greeted by the pungent stench of piss on one of the streets frequented by drunkards, the kind you see in all the small towns of the region. Her place was tiny. Her room was essentially a bed covered in stuffed animals and brightly coloured sheets, like a child's room. There were curtains separating her bed from the basic kitchenette, a table, two chairs, and a rickety stool. She shared a shower with the other occupants on her floor. The seediness of the place was all in the detail. There were empty bottles of wine piled up in crates or on the floor, dirty dishes everywhere, and an ashtray overflowing with cigarettes, most of them smudged with her bubblegum-pink lipstick.

'Will you have some wine, Jeanne?'

I sat on the wooden stool and watched her hand trembling as she poured me my first glass. I looked up and stared at her devoutly. She wasn't yet twenty-five and already her features were sunken. She avoided my gaze, as always. I could only ever imagine things about her because she never spoke to me about anything in depth. She couldn't. Like me, she was running from something inside her, always joking, always laughing with her loud and vulgar laugh.

My way of dealing with things, I felt, was more noble. The method I'd chosen to follow assiduously was to bury myself in books and schoolwork. It was a solitary, reclusive life, and it kept me going. I know now that my sense of pride kept me sane and satisfied. I couldn't bear the idea of anyone thinking I was easy, like she was. Flighty, maybe, but kind. Years later, when I came back for a trip down memory lane, I overheard two men talking in the bar: 'Remember Emma? You know, the blonde who used to work here. Pretty, a bit stupid. The one who would suck a dick for next to nothing.'

'Are you OK?'

'Not really.'

'What's wrong?'

'Shall I make some pasta?'

She was trying to change the subject. She got up, went to grab a pan, then stopped, arm outstretched. Without warning, her shoulders started shaking, her whole back convulsing with sobs. It broke my heart to see her standing there, crying noisily, but I was paralysed, incapable of consoling her. She sat down again, her face ravaged by sadness, streams of charcoal mascara ploughing down her face, and filled her glass to the brim.

'It's my fault. I bring it on myself.'

And so began the evening's hopeless confessions, past and present all jumbled into one. She'd fallen pregnant – 'an accident' – she was in love, she saw herself marrying him, this nice carpenter guy from the village in the valley.

She'd planned it all out for herself, a life lacking in any kind of originality: 'But you don't understand, he's so kind.'

How could I understand the word 'kind'? We'd gone through our entire lives knowing nothing of kindness, that elusive trait that would trouble my heart my entire life. He had told her to get an abortion, she was shocked, she'd thought he loved her too, they had, after all, recently spent a week together in Rimini.

'You don't just go away with someone for a week if you don't love them, do you? So I asked him what the problem was. Do you know what he said? Straight to my face? "I can't get married to the village tart."' More sobbing ensued, glasses were emptied one after the other. Then she got to her final point. 'Dad always said I was nothing but a little slut. He says I'm asking for it.'

That night, I finally saw what I'd been blind to all along. I'd never suspected a thing, never even had an inkling.

'It all started the night he hit you and the Doctor ended up coming. Do you remember?'

How could I forget?

'I mean, it didn't happen often. Maybe ten times.'

'What happened ten times?'

She was the one he made fun of at the table, the one he tried to humiliate in front of the few people we would meet, the one he called stupid. The one he raped.

'He raped you?'

'Raped? It wasn't rape exactly. I mean, I don't think so. More touching, kissing. Once, when I was a bit older, I gave him… I'm not going to spell it out for you. After that, he stopped.'

'Does Mum know?'

'Mum doesn't know anything. He said it was my fault. He said I was a tease and I did it on purpose. I swear I didn't do it on purpose. I already had boobs. He loved them.' That's what she said. *He loved them*.

'Are you out of your mind? Fathers aren't supposed to love their daughters' breasts. Do you hear yourself talking?'

'I know it's bad. But I was his favourite.'

It was despicable. Obscene. I couldn't breathe. I was filled with sorrow for her, hatred for him. More than ever. I thought of my mother, unable to hear, see or speak. My mother, who I worshipped and cherished. And this family, more wretched than I could have imagined. I wanted to console her, take away her pain. I couldn't. His favourite.

4

Lausanne was, more than anything, an escape. Even before I qualified as a teacher, I knew I would continue my studies. It wasn't a question of ambition. It was a way out. As chance would have it, my canton didn't have a university. Which meant I could move even further away from my family. If ten kilometres hadn't been enough to quell the hate and anguish, perhaps a hundred would do the trick.

My choice was as symbolic as it was vital. And in any case, how could I, at the age of twenty, have taught classes, organized meetings with parents? I was awkward, incapable of having normal relationships, unable to hold polite, everyday conversations. In short, I was a social misfit. Studying felt like the only way to weave a path between my anger and having some semblance of a normal life. It was the only way to survive.

Once in the city, I did all I could. I found a room on my own. One with a kitchenette and a bathroom with no door. A poky place void of any comfort. I got a grant for a meagre sum, an interest-free loan. I stumbled upon a job to make ends meet. I could never have worked in a bar. Too many people. I couldn't have worked in a shop. Too awkward. There just so happened to be a position going at the kiosk in the Sous-Gare district. All I had to do was listen, serve and hand people things over the piles of newspapers. In exchange for greeting and serving customers, I got anonymity. Saturdays plus a few hours during the week were enough to cover my shopping. Lausanne was a resurrection.

I discovered the impulsive joy of taking the Sion–Lausanne line. It was then, as the train pulled into Villeneuve, that I saw it for the first time. The lake. Hypnotic. Captivating. Whenever the train went by and I saw the water appear through the window, I would close my book. It didn't matter which book. Not even Paul Auster's *New York Trilogy*, which I devoured with blissful devotion, could compete with the grey-blue of the lake blending seamlessly into the sky on certain days. From the train, I would see the people walking along the docks, the Château de Chillon, the little boats moored a little further along. (One was always moored in the same spot, and for years I wondered who it might belong to.)

Many people appreciate the lake's simple, reassuring beauty. But I saw it as the witness to my transformation. It was my accomplice, and it was stunning. The foam on the lake let me know that from then on, my horizon stretched beyond the mountains of my childhood. I had learned to swim at fifteen and was the only one out of the whole school who had never been to a swimming pool. Within one term, I caught up thanks to a stubborn desire to learn all the things my father had forbidden us to do. The summer she became a teenager, my sister asked if she could go to the swimming pool in Sion with her friends. 'What for, to show your arse off to everyone? The pool is for whores!' he bellowed, three centimetres from her face. We never went on holiday. We'd never seen the sea, nor sand, nor pebbles. There was no Italian ice cream, no contagious laughter, no bright-orange beach flags or deckchairs.

I've come to love Lausanne for one main reason: Lake Geneva. The symbol of my exile. The people and buildings are a world apart from home. Things are richer in every sense of the term. The clothes, the hairstyles, the architecture, and all the different districts, each with its idiosyncrasies. No more whispering when I walk past people, no more staring or jeering, no more shame. It's like I'm a new person. Unseen, unnoticed. I slip into the cinema by myself in the afternoon, I wander through the steep streets, I look at the window displays of the luxury boutiques on Rue de Bourg and stumble upon the most beautiful department store I've ever seen, Bongénie, which I never dare enter. I go to exhibitions without understanding a thing because we never did that kind of activity growing up.

To begin with, I conquer the lake with my eyes. I walk along the banks from Ouchy to Lutry. I dream of jumping straight into the water, but I'm afraid. The only water I've ever been in is chlorinated pool water. When I finally muster the courage, my chest swells with intense joy. I'm happy, relieved to be so far from where I grew up. One hundred kilometres is nothing. But it's as though every kilometre adds a layer of veneer until eventually my origins are no longer visible. On the surface, at least. Over the weeks, I conquer Lake Geneva one stroke at a time. Each time, there's the shock, the tingling in my feet, my thighs and my stomach, before I bend my legs and glide through the water, arms outstretched. There's no one there to watch me, or praise me for my progress. *If Mum could see me…* I think sometimes. I imagine her there above me, looking on fondly, smiling, proud as punch. But I swim alone. I have my life, and they have theirs. The water tells me so in a whisper each time I vigorously kick my feet.

I let down my guard. My face relaxes into a smile when I pass people in the street. My shoulders soften, my eyes take in the facades of the buildings and their breathtaking grandeur. Classes begin; I start meeting others. There are people of all stripes: some are timid like me, then there's the cunning, the conceited, the class clowns and the sly foxes. For the first time, I get invited to a party by a group of fellow students who are sharing a flat. I laugh, get drunk. I find the courage to talk without overthinking. It's new, it feels strange, and it's fantastic. Everything is a first. Alcohol and music liven up these evenings, but so do the stories we share from childhood. Memories that remain fresh in my mind yet distant enough for me to not risk giving anything away. Especially inconsequential chatter about the books we read as children. *Fantômette*, *Sophie's Misfortunes*, *The Famous Five*: 'Which one were you?' 'Do you remember Colleen McCullough?' 'Are you kidding me?' 'They made it into a TV series. I was mad about Ralph de Bricassart…'

Despite my efforts to move on from the past, it keeps going for the jugular. The mere mention of Ralph de Bricassart takes me straight back to the family living room. My mother and I had read *The Thorn Birds*, and we were so excited about the novel being brought to life on television. It was the first time I'd seen characters from a book materialize outside of my own imagination. I would sit with my feet tucked beneath me, snuggled up to my mother, captivated by the story and the actor, Richard Chamberlain, who played the notorious priest caught up in the conflict between his carnal desires and the Church. My father drunkenly glanced up at the television from time to time. I remember the Sunday the second episode aired. Without warning, he started yelling at my mother: 'Is this shit making you wet, you little whore?' He continued to hurl nonsense at her, a thick white foam forming at the corners of his mouth. I already knew his anger would boil over before raining down onto my mother's hollow cheeks. We never watched the TV together again.

I hid all my sorrow from the others, I pushed it down inside where, little by little, it gnawed at my guts. These discussions quietly chipped away at my armour, but they did nothing to diminish my anger or shame. For so long, I'd been on the outside when it came to family, school, people in general. I'd always believed, pretentiously, that I was different. But now I realized that my extensive, haphazard literary escapades in the solitude of my room had laid the foundation for connecting with others despite myself. Deep down, I realized, I wasn't a complete outsider. That constant, nagging fear had not consumed everything. No matter how much drama, suffering and turmoil goes on within families, it doesn't necessarily show.

Still, this intense fear, a fear nobody will ever be able to appease, made a seasoned escape artist of me; I could duck out of any conversation if I sensed a heart-to-heart coming on. I was the weird girl. Thankfully, people put this down to me being from Valais, known for its unusual geography and its inhabitants' vehement and visceral attachment to their provincial attitudes and values, something my peers seemed to find endearing. Whenever I would sit there scowling or put on my jacket and scurry away in the middle of a discussion, someone would always pipe up with: 'Typical bloody Valaisian.'

Though I remained too cynical, too disillusioned, too wary and elusive to ever invest much in relationships, these light and cheerful encounters at university, far from home, kindled a spark of affection for where I was from. They unravelled my past just enough to make it bearable.

In the city, I could catch my breath; it was love at first sight. I pushed my family to the back of my mind and out of my life. After a while, it was as though they'd never existed. Sometimes, at night, as I took the few steps across my tiny room to get to the toilet, my sister's face would appear. My heart would race as I stood there in my underwear. I'd rush to find the switch, groping around in the dark. The light would calm the feeling of dread. And if it still wasn't enough to ward off the creeping sadness, I'd open a book and fall asleep with the bedside lamp on. My survival instinct was stronger than my family ties. My love for my mother was stagnating lifelessly somewhere deep inside.

It's only as I gradually stop obsessing over my family that it dawns on me. I'm captivated by women. I watch them in the bus, at the supermarket checkout. I sneak glances at them on the sly. Crossed, slender legs beneath translucent stockings, a smooth chest, flushed or speckled with moles. A slight hesitation, an alluring gesture, intentional or otherwise. I notice all the details they don't. Childlike freckles on faces, golden-brown highlights running through hair, a gently bitten bottom lip, smooth calves, chest rising slightly before a sigh, nail tips filed into almonds or squares. Despite these fervent, rigorous and scrupulous observations, I'm never able to decipher their codes. I can't understand them. I'm hasty and severe in my judgement, I try to sniff out spite, conceit or bitterness beneath their seductive artifices, which are no match for my obstinacy. I put people in boxes that correspond to my own subjective criteria. I don't make friends. I always let others take the lead.

She's not the type to turn heads. Marine is a glimmer of light on the horizon at dusk. At first you don't see it, then its flickering light catches your attention, until finally it's so bright you wonder how you never noticed it before. Marine: a comforting body and a round face like Romy Schneider's. I study her discreetly as she pulls her black woollen jumper over her head. I catch a glimpse of her milky skin, her arched back visible above worn-out jeans. My stomach is seized by desire, a completely unfamiliar sensation.

'How's it going?' she asks, addressing the group of six people sitting around the Formica table. A hug for Catherine, a friendly jibe at Stéphane, a kind or funny remark for the others. When she gets to me, she stops, intrigued. I see those hazel irises, flickering like flames. All my senses are on alert, stunned in the presence of this girl. It's the first time I've felt my heart beat this fast out of something other than fear. 'And you must be Jeanne.'

I'm startled by the idea of people talking to a stranger about me, the stranger's casual way of telling me so. She bends down to greet me with a warm kiss on the cheek, so slow it feels sensual. I knew my sister exuded a kind of raw, animal sensuality, but otherwise I had never understood concretely what sexuality was. She takes a chair and sits down next to me at the corner of the table, her knee brushing against mine. Her physical proximity is a detonator. I feel a sensation in my genitals that I quickly try to contain and repress.

That very night, I discover the rudiments of masturbation. It's the first time, despite my age. The learning process unfolds naturally and easily, in November, in Lausanne, which I've come to hate, because I can't swim in the lake any more. November in Lausanne brings with it a cold fiercer and more biting than any I have felt in the Valaisian mountains, known for their mild foehn winds. Here, the wind lashes my cheeks, the icy humidity penetrates my bones, leaving cracks in my lips and the joints of my fingers. November in Lausanne absolves all the others that came before it.

5

The radio alarm sounds in my dormitory room. I open my eyes. Something must have happened. Perhaps I've forgotten an important meeting; I can't remember. My brains have been scrambled by the alcohol and the unspeakable secrets my sister shared the night before. I feel nauseous. Last night's wine is repeating on me. I don't have time to think about my brain or my insides, I have to get to class.

Preoccupied by Emma's revelations, I don't listen to a word. I don't even notice when the nun teaching my French class stops to open the door to someone.

'Jeanne! The *directeur* wants to see you.'

I walk down the corridor, lost in thought. Those words are devouring me, like leeches in my brain. *I was his favourite*.

The director, a kindly, fatherly man with prematurely grey hair, welcomes me into his office. 'Take a seat, Jeanne.'

He's mumbling, and I realize it's something about my sister. 'What about my sister? What is it?' I'm already fearing the worst. 'Where is she?' Then I bolt.

'Jeanne! Wait!'

But I'm already gone, tearing down the path that runs perpendicular to the main road, which I cross without paying attention to the traffic. I run past the Tour des Sorciers like a woman possessed and continue to sprint across the Place de la Cathédrale beneath the majestic chestnut and maple trees. I can hear the leaves and the empty chestnut shells cracking in two beneath the soles of my trainers.

When I arrive, gasping for air, there's a black sedan ominously parked in the narrow pedestrian street like a large stain. Strangers, faces I know, gather around, hunched over, shaking their heads helplessly or murmuring: 'How awful.'

My sister's boss, a local with frazzled, strawlike bleached hair, deftly grabs me by the forearm before I manage to get through the doorway to the building. 'Don't go up there, Jeanne. Come to the bistro with me.'

I'm struck by the stark contrast between her affectionate, maternal voice, with its local lilt, and her outlandish clothing. I wrench my arm free from her thin, wrinkled hands and race up the crooked stairs two at a time. As I reach the top, I hear the words: 'My God.' The door is open, I can't see a thing, two police officers are blocking the landing. I slip between the two of them, they make a token attempt to hold me back. I go inside. Immediately, the air thickens as the weight of tragedy fills the entire space like cement.

She's lying on the floor, wearing the same clothes as last night. I can't see her face. Someone is bent over her. They pull me away, I try to fight. A man with a firm grip takes me by the shoulders; I follow his steps mechanically. He takes me to a cafe that's usually closed at this time of day. Someone offers me a drink, a hand strokes my back. I sit there, perched on a bar stool. There's movement outside, voices. I go to pull back the nicotine-stained curtain, ignoring the stranger's voice pleading: 'Don't.' There are two men carrying a black bag. One in front, one behind. A funeral procession. Tears come flooding down in silence, but inside I'm screaming. So that's all it is, a life. Just a black bag.

They're standing there on the other side of the cobblestone path, doubled over with grief. My father, hands in pockets. His head is hanging so low, all I can see is his bald skull. My mother, deathly pale, clutching at her grey cardigan, her hand over her mouth. I'm paralysed. Mum comes over to me, arms outstretched, I take refuge in them, softly we cry. Our chests rise and fall together in one united movement. Apart from our gentle sobs, there's not a sound. It's as though the city has emptied itself of all its usual noises.

Days pass, my body mechanically complies with its obligations. Death has a way of freezing the frame. Moments that seem insignificant at the time, snippets of banal scenes, remain forever imprinted in memory. Scenes of everyday life, stopped in its tracks, forming complete images. Scenes from past deaths blend into fresh grief.

A memory of me as a child, yet to experience the pain of bereavement. My late uncle's apartment is heavy with the reverential silence of mourning. His body is laid out in the centre of the room in an open coffin. I'm not afraid. If anything, it feels natural. I'm impressed by all the adults' grave expressions. My mother leads Emma and me outside. We hide under a set of stairs near a cellar that reeks of mould. She's crying in silence.

'What's the matter?'

'Nothing.'

'Why are you crying?'

'Because I'm afraid.'

The only thing I'm afraid of is my father. It's the first time in my life that death has presented itself, and it seems normal to me. I can't comprehend my mother's fear. But we're loyal to her, and she's an adult, so Emma and I believe her – death means fear.

Was my sister trying to frighten the life out of us all with her sudden death, or was it just to frighten him? Did she think she could give us a wake-up call to change things? Or was it that everything – being rejected, the abortion, the child that was never born – had plunged her into such a black despair that death was the only thing that could put an end to the pain? I can't accept that dying is the only way to stop suffering. It's too absolute. It means we've lost against our father. I can't accept that I was incapable of saving her.

Emma knew better than I did about the grief and guilt that come when death takes you by surprise. The night of my uncle's funeral, at supper, after paying our respects to a man we hadn't been close to, ten-year-old Emma made a remark, probably to break the heavy silence imposed by my father's presence: 'What an awful thing, to die.'

Our mother tried to comfort her. Our mother, who had confessed her own fears only a few hours earlier. But my father interjected: 'You think death is awful? Stupid girl! It's completely normal.' That exact moment, by some terrible coincidence, Micky the cat slunk cautiously past the doorway. My father and I, who were facing the kitchen door, spotted Micky at the same time. My father jumped up from his chair, rushed towards the creature, grabbed it by the scruff of the neck and held it firmly over the table, right in front of my sister's nose. 'You think it's awful that old bastard died? Answer me, stupid girl! You think it's awful? The cat was squirming for its life, thrashing in the air with its paws. My father grabbed Emma with his other and she had no choice but to follow him. I was frozen to the spot. I heard the water running in the bathtub, Emma's screams, the cat's shrill, piercing cries, my father's yells: 'Shut the fuck up, mog!' He drowned Micky. It took a long time, but he did it. He forced Emma to watch the whole thing, then bury her beloved pet at the bottom of the garden. He stood there with a beer in his hand, yelling 'Hurry up, stupid girl!' for the whole neighbourhood to hear. As usual, nobody did anything. By the time the whole thing was over, it was pitch-black outside. My mother had put me to bed. Through the bedroom wall, I could hear Emma's relentless sobs. Through the wall, I heard my father yanking off his belt. 'If either of you tries to do anything, I'll destroy the pair of you, too!' he shouted. Emma didn't speak again for a week.

*

I had to honour her decision. The choice not to take her secrets to the grave along with her body, so agonizingly alive and voluptuous only yesterday. The choice to not be an accomplice to that bastard. I went through the funeral on autopilot. The feelings, the photo of her, taken at least five years ago, propped up on the cheap wooden coffin, the village vultures who came to sprinkle some holy water while getting a good look at our grief-stricken faces. I didn't shed a single tear. And my mother: dignified, stiff, unreadable. I could feel the pain in her every movement. I had to endure watching the entire village, along with friends and acquaintances, hungrily making their way down the church aisle, like a centipede nibbling away at its prey, to bless my sister, nailed inside her coffin. All the while we just stood there, waiting idiotically with our heads bowed. Family members who hadn't seen Emma in years wore their best solemn expressions. I wanted to be alone, I begged my mother and the priest. Out of the question. Privacy is a mark of sin. To this day, obituaries are published alongside a portrait photograph on the last page of our local newspaper. At the time, either hypocrisy or Christian superstition would not allow the addition of a modest epitaph: *Left this world of her own free will.*

The whole village, known for its lack of solidarity and a propensity for spitefulness, had turned out in droves to revel in our public display of misery. Anger, my eternal companion, was tearing my stomach apart. I wish I could have held it together in public. I couldn't. As soon as I stepped out onto the church square, I exploded with grief. It wasn't pretty. It spoiled the solemnity of the moment. My memory, otherwise impeccable, infallible, has wiped away all trace of the monologue I spewed in my father's face that day. All I remember is an aunt I barely know, my mother's sister, dragging me away as I yelled: 'You raped her. You killed her.'

And with that, my final goodbyes to my sister came to an end at the top of those stone steps.

They took me back to the boarding school by force. I was thrashing about like a woman possessed, drooling and screaming. My aunt's husband slapped me. 'She must be having a nervous breakdown. Call a doctor.' A cousin came to stay the night with me. I drifted in and out of sleep, waking up in floods of tears. Dark nightmares would follow. My father is choking me, I'm gasping for air, I can hear screams, the boarding school supervisor shouts: 'I'm calling the police.' He's there in front of me, completely wasted. 'I'll kill you, you little bitch!' I lie there motionless, stupefied by the drugs. 'Never come back again or I'll kill you! Do you understand me, you dirty little whore?'

I didn't go back. Those words, probably the fruit of madness, hatred or pain, were words I decided to obey. I did everything to get away from them, from the mire sucking me in. I became steely and matter-of-fact, I went inside my shell. I finished my year, just about. I didn't invite them to my graduation. No thanks, no acknowledgement. Live or die. I'd made my choice.

6

I didn't know a thing about attraction, desire, or even my tastes. Nothing. At the age of twenty, I was completely indifferent to sex because I was impervious to all kinds of pleasure. Hypervigilance had taken over my entire existence. Mind and body. Day in, day out. Anticipating my father's actions, constantly being afraid. It's hard to imagine, living in fear every day. Every single day. Coming home from school wondering if he'd be there, if he'd be drunk, if he'd be angry. Holding my breath every time I heard the faintest noise, or worse, the sound of his voice, listening to the way he put on or took off his shoes, barely daring to breathe at the dinner table, in the bathroom, doing my homework, reading.

My body is a fortress: it doesn't know peace. My legs are always anxious to run away. My body is a radar for detecting my father's presence: neck bent, eyes fixed on what's in front of me, head and shoulders contracted; a buffalo's hump is all that's missing. My body hurts, and I deny the pain it causes me: heartburn and stomach ulcers at the age of twenty, a mangled back. My body doesn't exist, my body knows neither consolation nor pleasure. My body doesn't belong to me; my heart has been hollowed out. There's only one dream in my head, one hope in my mind, and it's stronger than me, than anything. I need to leave.

Much later, when I confessed to Marine that I had never had a single sexual thought during my teenage years, she gasped in shock. 'That's impossible! Everyone thinks about sex! Sex is life.'

I was born dead.

There was one girl, however, who threw me for a loop, soon after I'd moved to Lausanne, just after experiencing that fleeting spark of emotion for Marine. The girl was so far removed from everything I'd ever known, she didn't seem real. One day, as she casually removed her jacket in class, I spotted the label in the lining: Chanel. I didn't know a thing about clothing, but Chanel was another story. 'That's for rich people,' my mother would say, admonishing my sister as she flicked through the pages of the magazines a friend had lent her, cooing.

I was blown away by Charlotte, and she was intrigued by me. I could tell right away. From her voice, her mannerisms, the way she'd throw back her head whenever she laughed. She was fearless, she flirted (or at least pretended to) with everyone: teachers, men, women. She would disappear for days, and I'd later find out somehow or other that she'd been modelling in a photo shoot. All long legs and gangly limbs, she wasn't exactly what you'd call pretty. She had the face of a baby bird, a flat nose and deep-set eyes. Her allure had more to do with her upbringing, her background, the things she wore and the way she presented herself. They made her irresistible. But she was full of shit. She was like something out of a film. And films are nothing but make-believe. I should have known.

If Charlotte hadn't cornered me first, I would never have tried to approach her. When she showed an interest in me, I went along with it. I couldn't resist. She was living proof that no one could see the marks my father had left.

She came and stood right in front of me while I was eating a sandwich on a bench and brazenly started stroking my hair. Slowly, from the roots to the tip of my ponytail. I was stunned by the sheer nerve of it, rooted to the spot.

'Have you ever tried doing a hair mask?'

And just like that, our two worlds collided. I'd always been able to rely on my intellect, and now here she was, this smart, provocative girl (I knew she was smart because we took several classes together), talking to me as if we were at the hairdresser's. She sat down, grazing my arm (intentionally, I think), and started talking to me about my hair, serious as anything.

'Your hair's lovely, but you need to take care of it.'

I couldn't argue with her monologue. I didn't know how. I was both taken aback by her superficiality and petrified by her defiant attitude.

Charlotte could insert herself into any discussion, in any setting. She would switch from trivial to profound topics without batting an eyelid. She taught me to appreciate Beauty with a capital 'B' – her own pretentious (and frankly, ridiculous) words, not mine. She taught me to appreciate excellence without intellectual distinction, to recognize it in a coffee or a film, a vegetable or a novel. She came from one of those posh families I had read about and idealized in my imagination. I devoured her presence and poise with my eyes. I was fascinated by the way she held her wrist just so, the colour of her nail varnish, the triumphant angle of her chin, her delicate neck, which she purposely accentuated with a dancer's bun. I was bewitched by everything, from where she'd been born to the way she crossed her legs.. I fell in love with an image; she was proof I was moving up in the world.

'You have to fill yourself up with beauty,' she declared. 'Educate your senses. You learn by looking and touching. The same goes for people. It's the same thing. I've seen the real you, beneath the rags.'

Rags. She really did use that word.

She was scintillating, and I couldn't believe she was interested in me. She thought I was quirky and exotic. I think she made it her business to educate me. That was the mundane truth of the matter. Of course, I was taken aback when she took my face in her hands and kissed me, eyes wide open. It wasn't a passionate kiss. It felt too contrived, too theatrical. Instinctively, she sensed my fear, my lack of experience. She liked seeing herself reflected in the eyes of a virgin and knew exactly what she had to do. She ran her hand through my hair, her tongue along my neck.

'Everything about you is delicious,' she said. Her mouth continued its conquest of my body with something closer to academic application than great enthusiasm. I relished the faint crackle of excitement in my belly. I closed my eyes to smell her body, more intoxicated at the idea of having conquered my own past than I was by her.

I knew nothing of sweat mingling on warm skin, I didn't know you could kiss eyes, lick breasts, grab buttocks, I had never imagined you could bury your nose in an armpit, your tongue in a vulva. I knew none of that, and deep down I didn't care. I was cold. I was pretending, overacting, imitating Charlotte. I liked the idea of it all, but my body felt nothing. I liked the aftermath, the nights when our legs intertwined, her gentle breath on my neck. I liked this new closeness. I liked that she liked me.

Before long, I abandoned my shabby studio to go and live with her. In everything she did, necessity and superficiality became one and the same. Snorting to herself, she would flatly proclaim: 'Linen sheets are for summer, Egyptian cotton is for winter.' I lapped up her cooing, flattered that a girl like her could like someone like me. In the evening, she'd light candles in our one-bedroom flat on Avenue de France ('A little candlelight can transform even a supper of bread into an elegant feast'). With that, she would take her copy of *In Praise of Shadows* and grandiloquently read aloud a passage to prove she wasn't shallow. She'd dig out an old cotton sheet – or better, linen – and use it as a tablecloth. She'd stick a branch in a glass bottle to add a bit of ambience to the room. She'd pick up an old bit of furniture in the street when the neighbours were having a clear-out, strip the wood and fiddle about with it until its former glory was restored. It wasn't until later that I understood that she was doing the same thing with me: stripping me bare so she could make me into something more acceptable. We were completely ridiculous, an unlikely pair shut away together, each of us a sticking plaster for the other's wounds, although we weren't aware of it. And so it continued: I traded in my polyester jumpers in favour of better-quality fabrics ('At least buy merino, you can always get cashmere later'), hunted for leather shoes that wouldn't cost the earth, a well-cut pair of jeans, until I could finally hold my head high and feel a little less like a pauper. The vacuity of it all diverted my attention from my torments and provided a welcome distraction. This early intimation of what attraction might mean bolstered my ego.

One spring morning, having tamed my hair with fancy shampoo or a concoction of egg yolk and oil she'd given me, my eyelashes thick with mascara, I caught myself simpering at a shop assistant. Thanks to my new look, nobody could have ever guessed where I'd come from. Nobody could have imagined there were abandoned car wrecks piled up in front of my childhood home, that people used to say 'Here she is, the little street rat' when I walked past, that the whole house stank of my father's cheap wine. With every layer of gloss I added to my appearance, I felt my anger subsiding, my past fading away. Charlotte had stripped it all away until I lost myself.

When I walked out of the shop that day with my shopping bag, for a few seconds I felt exultant, my chest swelling with pride. I didn't get far before it hit me: I was disowning my family. And that meant disowning my mother. I felt a visceral hatred for her, the way she'd readily taken on the role of the victim. I resented her for not having escaped to protect us. When I was eight years old, after that fateful beating, I had screamed at her: 'Why don't we just leave this house?' She looked down at the ground and back up again, eyes full of tears, and shrugged. 'And go where?' Her hands were tied. She had no qualifications, no idea another life was possible. I, on the other hand, knew all about the good life now.

I thought about the spectacle I'd made of myself in the fruit and vegetable aisle and was choked with guilt and shame. It had been four years since I'd last set foot in the little mountain village I'd once called home. After my sister's funeral, after seeing my mother's grief, after the scene I'd made, I'd severed all ties. Not a single phone call, letter or card. I'd made a clean break, as they say.

Charlotte had only a vague idea about my former life. My affection for my mother, my hatred for my father, snippets from scenes of horror I'd played down for her benefit. Memories, exaggerated and embellished, of the hours I'd spent daydreaming with my notebook or reading late into the night.

The time had come to return to the fold. I didn't have to think twice. The second I closed the door behind me, I announced that I would be going to visit my mother that Saturday afternoon.

'I'll go with you.'

'No, I'd rather go alone.'

'I want to see where you grew up! I want to see your house and meet your mum.'

'She doesn't even know what a lesbian is.'

'We'll say we're good friends. I'm coming with you and that's that!'

On the Monday, I call my mother when I think my father will be at work. The phone rings once, then twice. My heart is pounding. After the first ring, I hear her voice.

'Hi, Mum.'

'Oh, Jeanne!'

I can hear her tearing up, and my chest swells with the love I've disregarded all this time. It's settled. I'll see her on Saturday at three. 'Will he be there?'

'I don't know. I'll tell him you're coming. I have to.'

When Saturday morning comes around, Charlotte is champing at the bit; I'm overwhelmed by emotion and fear. We board the train which takes us past the lake, that dazzling spectacle I never tire of. The glistening blue of the water that blends seamlessly into the sky. I tell Charlotte I wish I could jump through the window and dive in. She hates water. For her the lake's value is solely aesthetic, nothing more than a quintessentially Swiss postcard. She'll never know how much of my sorrow it's washed away. For the first time, I realize how empty our relationship is. I attribute this first tinge of doubt to the stress of going back to that house.

At the station, we catch the postbus that takes us about ten kilometres up the winding road leading to the village. It's an epic adventure for my travel companion, who has never set foot in one of these bright yellow vehicles that zigzag across rural Switzerland.

As always, she's rabbiting on to fill the silence. 'I simply adore the Valais region.'

'Charlotte, we haven't been here five minutes. What do you know about Valais?'

'I happen to know it rather well! I've been skiing several times in Zermatt, as a matter of fact. My mother insisted on getting a Range Rover for our first stay in Crans-Montana. We were only there a week! She was being crazy and hysterical as usual.'

I think of my mother, counting the pennies to feed us, mending our clothes, selling our books so she could buy us more. I feel myself getting disproportionately angry. I want to shout in her face. What do you know about Valais, Charlotte? There are hundreds of unpretentious places here, completely untouched by anything except nature, that would move your heart if only you had one. What do you know about the rustic Val d'Hérens, or the wild hamlet of Forclaz, which may not have any touristy restaurants but will force you to confront your own soul as soon as you set foot there? There isn't just one Valais. People living mere kilometres apart each have different accents, look after their own little piece of land, which they consider the most wonderful treasure on earth. And the girl from first year at university, do you remember her? She came from Martigny, a windy city where, according to her, the water tastes better than anywhere else. Did you know there are apricot trees that grow only in specific spots, and farmers who, afraid of losing their livelihoods to the frost, take painstaking care of them as they burst into blossom? And the cold nights, when they place heaters at the roots of the trees, and the glistening light of the early morning that's enough to make you cry. How touching to know there is a man keeping watch over every last shrub, that the silt from the river Rhône gives the asparagus its unique flavour. Did you know there are as many hours of sunshine in Sion as there are in the South of France? That there are spots where the Barbary fig grows? Did you know they can produce two harvests each year if the tree is planted facing the sun, or even better, against a wall? I know. My favourite professor at teaching college, Rachel, would bring them in by the armful. There's simply no comparison between the first time I bit into a fig freshly picked from the tree and the fruit buffet in your five-star restaurant on that mountain you know nothing about. Because the mountain is harsh, its avalanches breed sorrow, the mountain roads are winding and show no remorse for speed or inebriation; they took the lives of five kids from my village, barely out of their teens, a stone's throw away from my house. Yes, we're less sophisticated than you, as you've told me many times, yes, our language is coarse and improper. Yes, we use words nobody outside our canton can understand. But my dear, when you have a father like mine, a vile man dead set on destroying your life, it's precisely those little things that give you your identity. Because I don't have a family identity. Your home may have been packed to the rafters with books. You may have been given education and culture. You may have had the luxury of never worrying about money. But look at yourself, Charlotte. You're modelling in fashion shoots, you'll never finish school, and your brother is set to take over your father's business. And what will you do then? Did it ever occur to you that you might be the one who's backward? You'll marry a man like your father, you'll get a facelift like your mother, and you'll buy moon boots you'll only wear twice, and you'll paint your nails, and you'll put on your lipstick, and you'll climb into your great big Jeep and drive to this region you claim to know. As for me, I will never set foot in Zermatt for as long as I live.

Of course, I said nothing. Back then I didn't have a good word to say about my home.

It wasn't until I went back with her that I understood: her sophisticated upbringing, which I'd been so impressed by, was completely lacking in any kind of substance or authenticity. She had no roots. It would take time for me to realize that the sophisticated family of hers I so coveted was worth no more than my brute of a father.

As we make our way around the hairpin bends, she's gushing like a madwoman about the driver's 'mastery' of the roads, which is simply 'insane'. I'm horrified that she's more interested in the scenery than how I'm feeling, that she can't seem to sense the fear ravaging my stomach. The landscape is just as I left it, as if it were yesterday: a smattering of villages separated by vineyards and dry meadows. I'm not yet able to feel any tenderness towards the villages

I desperately wanted to forget. They're too intricately linked to my past. I'm lacking the distance I need. It'll be a long time before I get it.

Our stop. My heart is beating harder and harder as we make our way through the village to get to the one house that's isolated from all the rest. I remember skipping along this road to get to school. The narrow 'streets' are not so much streets as roads without pavements, roads we'd walk along as kids three or four times a day, pressing ourselves up against the walls each time a vehicle passed without slowing down. Sometimes we'd get soaked by a car going full throttle through a puddle without a care in the world. In winter, so much snow would fall that all the kids would go out in the road on Wednesday afternoons and ski. Emma and I had a sled. Skiing equipment was far too expensive. Dogs would turn nasty from being tied up outside all year long. There were a lot of deaf people in my village. 'Consanguinity,' explained a science teacher who came from out of town. 'Belgian prick!' yelled my father when Emma relayed the explanation to him. A carpet of primroses lined the embankments. I would pick fistfuls of them for my mum. They'd be limp by the time I handed them to her, but she'd give them some semblance of life for a day or two by putting them in an old jam jar. Then there were the snails we collected in tins but – thankfully – never ate because my father didn't like them. Instead, we'd deliver them to a man in the village in exchange for two francs.

I vaguely hear Charlotte telling me she feels as though she's 'in a Tuscan village', asking me questions as details come spontaneously flooding back, brought to life by the smells and by the route I used to take as a child. What if we hadn't had him as a father? Would we have been happy? Would I still have wanted to run away?

After ascending the steep hill, we take a final turn, and I recognize the age-old walnut tree we used to climb, the one my mother asked a neighbour to build a swing on, and I can still smell that scent I loved of walnut husks being cracked between fingers to reveal the fresh nut inside. The pebbly path. The worm-eaten fence that's barely standing.

And Mum, sitting there on the bench.

7

Charlotte was so dazzling in her appearance it almost verged on tacky. Yet I was blinded by it. It was violence; plain, distinct, clear as day. Her scheming and artifices were far removed from everything I knew. I was bowled over by how she behaved, how she'd been brought up, the exuberant childhood featuring live-in staff, the kind of holidays reserved for only the upper echelons of society, on islands I wouldn't have been able to place on a map. What an honour to be her chosen one. My strong intuition, which rarely failed me when it came to judging whether I liked people, be it for their nature, intellect or kindness, had been dulled by her bourgeois duplicity.

When I had first arrived in Lausanne, the cheerful crowd who had welcomed me with open arms and without judgement had pulled me out of my withdrawal and solitude. But over time, the group began to drift apart. I put it down to us having gone in different directions, to the fickleness of youth. The gatherings became less and less frequent as the months passed. One of the group quit his studies to take on freelance work that eventually led to a newspaper job, another started art school. Even Marine, sweet, bubbly Marine who had made such a big impression on me, who flitted from one group to the next and was friends with everyone, had fallen off the radar.

I was still working at the kiosk one block away from the train station when one Saturday in October, just before I finished work, I heard that unmistakable bright laugh. My heart leaped; I tried to spot her. She was standing on the other side of the street, talking to a couple and waving at me. She came over, leaned across the newspapers and planted one single, noisy kiss on my cheek before inviting me for a drink at the Italian place on Boulevard de Grancy.

When we get there, she orders wine. She talks and talks, about her training as a social worker, about the LGBT activism she's involved with, about her volunteering, and about me – she often thinks about me. I have no control over what's happening between us. There's clearly some kind of osmosis taking place at a rate too fast for my discretion to handle. Still, I exercise caution and restraint. She asks me about Charlotte. 'Watch out for that one,' she tells me firmly.

'What for? She's so...' I rack my brains for an adjective and opt for the most banal, boilerplate term that comes to mind. '...great.' Once I've said it aloud, it doesn't sound right.

'Be careful, that's all. I don't want you to get hurt.' And with that, she flashes me a wide smile and runs towards the station in her big boots.

*

Back in my mother's kitchen, a memory, like a consolation, is superimposed on Charlotte's obnoxiously posh laugh. You can't laugh like that in a shabby kitchen when you grew up in a mansion by a lake, raised by a nanny. You can't laugh like that in front of a woman withering away in an old-fashioned dress that's too formal for a Saturday afternoon. You can't laugh like that in the face of the fading, greenish tinge of a black eye. Yet there she is, laughing, to the point where it almost feels rude. She reminds me of those rich tourists who trill gleefully about how 'wonderfully authentic' things are the minute they set foot in an impoverished region where they'll never live. She finds the coffee cups 'gloriously old-fashioned', the curtains 'so very romantic'. When she spots the wooden table, she asks: 'Valaisian, I assume?'

It was there in the kitchen that it dawned on me. She had chosen me to escape from her roots. Just like I had chosen her. I realize that despite the denial, despite the antics we've each forced ourselves to perform as part of our respective metamorphoses, our origins have left their eternal, indelible mark. You can see it whenever we feel uncomfortable, or conversely, when we let our guards down. No matter how hard we might try to fight it, Charlotte will always say 'damn when I say 'fuck'.

I'm not capable of hugging my mother. I'm not capable of rubbing her back. I can't hold her hand, even though it's inches from my own. I'm made of stone. It pains me to see her cautious, modest glances, the love in her eyes that

I don't know how to return. I'm ashamed to have pushed her so far down in my memory, in my shrivelled heart.

The door slams shut. My throat contracts when I hear his clumsy footsteps on the floor tiles.

'You made it then.'

That's all he says. I look at him. My childish impudence has vanished. I try to reason with myself. He's not going to kill all three of us. Four years have passed, but looking at him, you'd think it was ten.

His presence is as imposing as I remember. The sound of those four words in succession is all it takes for the past to come flooding back. My shoulders tense, my movements become robotic. I'm glued to my chair, unable to get up. Charlotte comes back from the bathroom and says hi to him, as though he were just a normal person. He is, to her. Just an oaf who commands respect by virtue of being under his own roof.

She works her magic. She looks at him, smiles sweetly and holds out her hand. 'Jeanne told me a lot about you,' she coos.

I watch the scene unfold as though watching a play. I see the hollow, insincere politeness she's been brought up with. I see the way she coaxes and soothes people to make them like her. And she certainly does it well. I haven't even told her a fraction of the story: the way he'd drag them across the room by their hair, the touching (it will be years until I'm able to use the word 'rape'), my mother's muffled screams, their bed banging against the wall like a metronome beneath his weight.

Charlotte continues to beguile him. He awkwardly offers her something to eat. He's pathetic. He starts asking her questions: 'Ah. So you and Jeanne are doing your studies together? Yes, she's always been a clever girl.'

I take advantage of the distraction to grab Mum's hand under the table. I give it a little squeeze. Her hand is sticky. She smears Vaseline on her hands and feet because it's cheap and effective. There's a silent complicity between us; we share a hole in the heart. It's unbearably sad, so I clear the dishes and manage to drag Charlotte away as she spews out promise after promise about when they'll next meet.

My teeth remain clenched for the entire journey back. My jaw contracts, shifting from left to right as if to try and assuage the guilt, the remorse. I'm digesting my sadness and coming to terms with having seen Charlotte's mediocrity for the first time. I'm shocked by how petty our relationship is. All the while, she pesters me, oblivious to the hard, irrevocable realization I've come to. 'What's the matter? It's not that bad. Your parents' place is bucolic. Say something, Jeanne, I want you to talk to me. Please tell me what the matter is.'

Then come the tears. Crocodile tears I suppose, rolling down the pink Guerlain powder on her cheeks. She starts simpering, then muttering, then finally she loses her temper while struggling to keep up with me on the Pont Chauderon, upset by my silence and my long, resolute strides.

I slam the bedroom door and collapse onto the bed. I'm enraged and crushed in equal measures.

'Seriously, Jeanne, don't you think you're blowing this out of proportion? I've been through tough times too. Everyone has a difficult childhood. You know my dad cheated on my mum, you know that she ended up spending a fortune on plastic surgery and clothes in the hopes he'd be attracted to her again. Can you imagine what that must have been like?'

It's pathetic. I've heard it too many times before. I turn to her and scream: 'STOP! Shut the fuck up!' I'm standing there, fists clenched so tight I can feel my nails digging into the fleshy pads of my hands. She's taught me the coquetry, the airs and graces, but it's all been for nothing. I, on the other hand, have conquered the lake all on my own, treading its shores daily until I know my way around it with my eyes closed. I'm strong. I leap towards her and start shaking her.

Two seconds don't seem like a long time. But these two seconds unfold at an agonizing pace. She curls up into a ball and covers her head with both arms. I shake and shake her. Harder and harder. Two seconds. I see my father punching my mother's back as she curls into a ball on the floor. I'm him. My insides have turned to fire. There's no going back. I want to release my grip on her bony shoulders. I can't do it. I'm a spectator participating in the action despite myself. She's pushed me to my wits' end with her theatrical monologue, her artificial ways, her rehearsed speeches, her endless words. I'm a fly caught in her trap. I'm the moth, she's the dazzling allure of a lamp that shines too bright. Two seconds.

Her body rocks back and forth to the rhythm of me coming to my senses. I'm screaming and spitting. The embodiment of my father's brutishness. 'You're going to shut your mouth now, I've fucking had it with you, do you hear me? Spiteful bitch!'

She's in the foetal position. Finally, I hear her. 'Stop, Jeanne. Please stop.'

Only her pleading can put a stop to my movements. I'm no longer in control of them. I hold her in my arms. 'I'm sorry, I'm so sorry, I didn't mean it.'

We pick ourselves back up as though we've just been in an accident. It's as though there's a haze covering everything, there to underline the rawness of the scene. A fog filling our heads, tears spilling everywhere. I'm ashamed. Even more so when I see her staring at me, eyes wide and ravaged with despair. She goes into the bathroom and takes a bath. I hear her sniffing loudly through the wall. I fall asleep cocooned in the duvet. I wake up to her gently stroking my side. I can smell her orange-blossom cream. She caresses me and talks to me the way you talk to a child. She covers me in kisses mingled with tears, in my hair, on my forehead. She takes my face in her hands and kisses me for a long time. I kiss her back, languorously, and by the end we're both naked, stroking and licking each other ferociously. Without an ounce of love from my side.

8

The first time I felt tenderness was with Paul. I wasn't looking for it. I felt it like an embrace, this new feeling. It came uninvited, at the wrong time and in the wrong place, one morning in September. A friend had recommended me for a job, and the prospect of getting an interview through connections alone made me uneasy. I was bracing myself for arrogance (very à la mode in advertising companies back then), a tête-à-tête with one of those pretentious types who reek of vanity and Dior Fahrenheit. Expectations were low. I could already imagine the job: stupid, utterly useless. I was grumbling over breakfast that morning: 'I'm only going because I've been unemployed for over a year now. Else there's no way I would…' But Paul Leone (Italian, I imagined, from his surname) caught me off guard with his gentle, almost provincial simplicity. I was completely thrown by his charming manner, the lines that fluttered at the corners of his pale eyes every time he smiled. And he smiled a lot. It was all brand new. I was shaken by the immediate attraction I felt to this soul – a man's soul. I should have turned down the position. It would have made my life easier.

I'd decided to quit teaching once and for all, and the job was a godsend. Without a family, I devoted myself completely to my work with the same almost aggressive dedication as I had my studies. I wasn't a particularly warm teacher, but I cared about those kids. After a few years of working supply, I was finally offered a position. It always annoyed me when the kids didn't hand in their homework, so at the beginning of the school year I promised a reward: a trip for everyone who managed to complete all the tasks I set. The *directrice* gave me the go-ahead, on the condition that I finance the trip and arrange for my colleagues to take in the stragglers for the day.

There was one mummy's boy who gave me nothing but grief from day one. He'd answer me back in the most unbearably haughty way. He had a gift for trying my patience and was smart enough to do it surreptitiously, without breaking any school rules. When I had to call his parents into school once, they made it clear to me that he was God's gift and must never be spoken ill of. By the time June came around, he was one of the lucky four who passed the homework challenge. The week before our trip, he came up to my desk at the end of class with a defiant look on his face. I put on my best fake smile and raised my eyebrow in an expression of enquiry.

'I bet you're happy you'll be spending the whole day with me,' he said.

'Congratulations. You played by the rules.'

He flashed me a cocky smile, the smile of someone who always gets what they want. 'I made sure I didn't miss a single assignment. I just had to spoil the day for you.'

What was it about that devious talent he had for belittling me? Somehow, he made me feel like I was that little girl again, the little girl with a dictator for a father.

I pulled myself together. I'm an adult now, I thought, and I don't have to answer to anyone. Thanks to that kid, for the very first time in my life I gave myself the joyous pleasure of exercising the privilege that came with my position. Before I opened my mouth to speak, I thought for a few seconds about that fateful phrase, the phrase I hadn't dared utter since. This time, fear would not get the better of me. I was in my rightful place. And I had earned it.

'Well, my dear friend, I'm afraid you just lost your right to go on the trip.'

He began to protest vociferously: 'You can't do that!'

I folded my arms. 'I said you're not coming.'

After he left, slamming the door with an energy only children that age are capable of mustering, I collapsed into my chair, head in my hands. It wasn't that I'd got any satisfaction from belittling that little brat. But I'd dared to stand up to a know-it-all whose brand of toxic behaviour played on my weaknesses without him realizing it. That little mummy's boy had it coming. Except Mummy was a lawyer, and so was Daddy. With money, status, power, and a whole lot of pretension. Within the hour, they were on the phone, not to complain but to threaten me. Either their son was coming or they'd press charges. On what grounds, they couldn't say. 'But we'll find something if we look hard enough,' the father told me. 'We can always find something.'

All that fuss for one little shit who knew how to wrap adults around his little finger. Of course, he hadn't told them what had actually happened. The next thing I knew, I had a meeting in the head's office. I didn't have the energy to fight. It was the little shit's word against mine. I'd always tried to fight for justice, for what's right: morality, dignity and respect. But apparently I was nothing but a lousy teacher, a peasant fighting against the better sort. I wasn't the first he'd tried to wind up; my colleagues were beside themselves. They offered to call their own lawyer friends to advise me. No sir. I packed my things and left. I admitted defeat. Hands up. I didn't have the strength or the ammunition within me to fight back.

It was a major but surprisingly easy decision to leave the profession I had believed to be my life's vocation. Though the decision wasn't too painful, it coincided with a break-up. A few months earlier, I had finally ended things with Charlotte. Since the 'incident' two years prior, our relationship had become a festering, toxic environment and there was nothing either of us could do about it. With my monstrous father and her bitter mother, we were simply reproducing what we knew.

Marine and I had been meeting up ever since we'd run into one another at the station kiosk. Over time, she had come to know everything about my family. She listened with a tenderness I had never known, stroking my hand whenever I couldn't find the words. She wasn't inquisitorial like Charlotte. She didn't try to force me to get over my grief. And she told me her stories as well. She was more open and less troubled than I was. But despite her natural warmth, there was a reserve about her that reassured me. We'd sit on a terrace, smoke until there was no air left in our lungs, drink a few glasses of red wine, then go our separate ways after embracing. It took time before I could open my arms to her. Before I let myself feel the weight of her bosom against my own pubescent chest. Before I could bury my nose in her hair and linger there. Once we'd said goodbye, I'd go back to Charlotte, and I wouldn't answer her when she quizzed me about my weekly escapade. My father had his Sundays, I had my Saturdays.

The day the ritual ended was the day we broke up. Standing there with my chin on Marine's shoulder, I opened my eyes and looked across the street. Charlotte was there, right next to the Asian grocery store. Tense, motionless. Marine turned around and waved at her, then immediately left. For a moment I didn't move. I had to think fast, like a cheetah, to prepare for the inevitable scene. Of course, she went into full diva mode. The biggest drama queen of all time. All she needed was a diva's golden gown.

Her, sulking, a single tear running down her cheek. Me, stroking her arm, her, screeching: 'I knew you were cheating on me with that little bitch!' Two hours of I love yous, I hate yous, tears and threats. Me eventually saying: 'I swear I never cheated on you.'

'Whatever. You're just like your father.'

That one hurts. And she knows it. It's as if she's been waiting months to say it. It's a nasty, definite, direct comparison to my father's mysterious Sunday escapades, during which I always suspected he was cheating on my mother.

The slap released months of tension. I planted it right on her cheek. Along with the red mark came the regret. She shouted herself hoarse for ten minutes, a string of reproaches punctuated by sobs. The police came after the neighbours complained. I hung my head the as they asked, clumsily: 'Do you want to file a complaint, Madam?' I must have looked like a monster, standing there at almost six feet tall, towering over Charlotte's slender frame. She looked up at them like butter wouldn't melt and whispered that it was no big deal, that they could leave, that she was sorry.

I shoved a few things in a bag. She grabbed the sleeve of my leather jacket, clung to my shoulder, threw her arms around my neck. We were like wild animals, sizing each other up, protecting our own turf. I made it clear in case she hadn't already understood: I refused to remain stuck in this perverse relationship.

I called Marine from a phone box.

'Come over.'

No questions, no judgement. With her address in hand, I made my way to hers, crying. I cried until the tears dried up. Years of sorrow came flooding out in the space of two days, on her sofa, in her bed. I didn't hold back. I told her about the slap, about that first act of violence. It was a case of talking or dying a slow death. So I talked. And she didn't leave. She stayed at my bedside like a nurse, accommodating all the disgust I felt for myself. She accepted me without judgement, she taught me complete acceptance and genuine empathy, something I was never able to exercise myself. Love without frills, tender gestures, natural feelings, the liberation of the body. She was in tune with her sexuality, a *bon vivant*, a person of integrity, generous and giving, tender, alluring, sensual. She did things with genuine abandon. There was no calculating, no fear. Being next to her body and feeling her expansive love was like coming in from the cold. It was thanks to her that I gradually reconnected with my mother. I started going back to the village. I'd stay for two hours at the most. But I was able to go. As long as Marine came with me.

9

Paris, in March. I'd often have to come for work. It took a while to get used to. The city made me feel gauche and out of place, and I was too in awe to love it unconditionally. I wandered from one street to the next, getting lost somewhere on an avenue then ending up in a covered arcade from another era or a ramshackle bistro, always roaming with the same curiosity, always in complete anonymity, the way I liked it. Over time, Paris, and the impossibility of ever knowing everything about it, swept me off my feet.

Invariably, when I arrive at Gare de Lyon, whether the sky is overcast or speckled azure blue, I stand beneath the glass covering and light a cigarette. The ritual is a decompression chamber between my home and the city. With each exhalation of smoke, I cut myself loose of all my ties. I have the same ritual for the way back: standing, smoking, taking in all the unfamiliar sounds and smells, a fuzzy ball of sadness in my heart that unravels by the time I cross the border into Vallorbe, that curious municipality.

In Paris, I never set foot in the clothes shops, though I sometimes go into the department stores for fun. Whenever I can, several times a day, I sit on a terrace, never tiring of the colourful spectacle of the streets, reminding me I'm not from here but allowing me to believe I could be. These solitary excursions are always accompanied by pangs of sweet melancholy.

Inevitably, at some point or other, I end up thinking about my mother, who has never left her village. I greedily devour all the things she'll never know she's missing. The Seine in the early morning, the waiters in their black aprons, the aimless strolls of which I never tire, the heady scent of the flower shops I pass on the way. I think: If only you could see them, Mum, the flowers in Paris. No one will ever be able to comprehend the effect those elegant boutiques have on me, whether grand or modest, chic or rustic. We never had a flower shop in our village, but there was one in the capital of the canton, in a pedestrian street not far from the bookshop. Mum would look longingly at the window display without ever daring to enter. At home we had tulips, dahlias, peonies that were almost red in colour, but never any roses – too delicate.

Lemon balm, rosemary and lovage sprang up in plant pots beneath the kitchen windows. As soon as the first shoots broke through the earth, she'd go out in the mornings, when my father was not around, and walk from one cluster of flowers to the next, bending down to touch them. I watched her from the window, thinking she'd lost her marbles. Sometimes she was smiling, other times I could see her lips moving. I don't know what she felt, standing barefoot on that ordinary piece of land of ours, but I know she worshipped those few minutes each day. So no, no one, especially not the inhabitants of this city, could ever understand how a bouquet of lilies or a bunch of violets can bring me to tears.

When I have time, I head to the Chapel of Graces of the Miraculous Virgin on Rue du Bac. Since my childhood, I've never known how to pray. So many times I begged God to help me, but He never answered my pleas. My mother would bless us every night, tracing a cross on our foreheads which she sealed with a kiss, or drop a medal in our pockets – and later, our wallets. We were never told the story behind those medals. Mum simply reproduced gestures passed on through habit or superstition. She seemed impressed when I told her much later about the origins of those charms. Marine used to say Paris was an aggressive place. But all I could see was its beauty, its dazzling allure, its quaint little nooks and crannies.

On one of my jaunts, I discovered a tiny shop with crooked walls that could have been built a hundred years ago or just yesterday. The inside was filled with ceramics, works of art in their own right. It was rustic and lavish all at once. I was mesmerized by this unpretentious place that commanded deference simply by existing. I bought three cups for an outrageous price. If Mum or Marine had found out how much they cost, they'd have put them on display like works of art, or yelled at me. I left the shop and dawdled along the street, grinning from ear to ear, emboldened by my extravagance. I never told anyone, not even Marine, but over time, Paris proved to me that I had successfully extricated myself from my village and my father's clutches.

Somewhere between Rue Saint-Honoré and my hotel on Rue Jacob, Paul unexpectedly popped into my mind. In the years since I'd met him, something had awoken in me, an almost animal infatuation that I'd been trying my best to keep under wraps. In the pretentious environment of those offices belonging to his in-laws, he was as much of an outsider as I was. I overheard rumours in the corridors that his wife kept him under her thumb financially. But I never listened to office gossips. He was gentle and reassuring and had none of that raging testosterone I was running from. He hired me on the spot. We hit it off right away; a sort of silent, reciprocal complicity was established between us immediately. I hadn't seen it coming, this attraction to him that was unfamiliar, haunting. No one had ever had that effect on me before. No one ever would again, though I didn't know it yet. My body sensed it long before I did.

Before going out to while away the evening in the neighbourhood, with dinner at the Pré aux Clercs brasserie and soaking up the atmosphere at La Hune bookshop – which to my delight was open at night! – I lay down on the bed in the cramped room in the roof. I conjured up fanciful scenes in my sleep. It was the first time I had allowed myself to have erotic fantasies about Paul. The pleasure came all at once.

Something clicked for me during that intimate reverie. My relationship with Marine was deep and solid, but now I realized there was another way of loving. I hadn't shared those spectral images with anyone, yet they had been so dense, so powerful. From then onwards, I was finally able to breathe easily, something that hadn't been possible since childhood. I was coming alive.

Though we only lived metres from the station, when I got back, Marine was waiting for me on the platform, bubbling with excitement. That night, emboldened by my secret desire for Paul, I felt my body tremble like never before. On the train home, a phrase in a magazine I was reading had caught my eye: *Hard to please*. I was. And not only in the physical sense. The joys of life had been kept from me, under lock and key. The only exception was swimming, which I had only discovered once I was far away from my father. Everything else led back to him. Even basic needs, like eating or sleeping, harboured potential danger. I wolfed down my food and always slept with one eye open. Even singing was off limits.

My father had a radio for listening to the news and would mumble his reactions to the reporters' comments or the white noise being emitted, depending on the location of the device. When I was fourteen, Mum and I were singing at the top of our lungs one late afternoon, delighted because we knew the chorus of a song often played on the air. I swayed by her side as she cooked, our voices interwoven with the voices of Pierre Bachelet and his choir:

In the north they had their houses
Beneath their feet the coal
The sky was their horizon
They were miners, heart and soul.

We were careful. We always listened out for him. But we didn't realize his car had broken down that day and a colleague had dropped him off. We never heard him come in. First, he smashed the radio against the wall, then he grabbed Mum by the hair with both hands, shaking her furiously. 'You want to dance, you old hag? You want to dance, do you?' Deafening silence. Blood pulsing through my ears. He confiscated all our joys. He massacred all our pleasures.

10

In the early days of our relationship, Marine encouraged me to start seeing a therapist. It was 1 December, a date I remember because it was World Aids Day and I was wearing a red pin on my jumper. The man, much older than me, was dressed to the nines in a black three-piece suit. After that first fifty-minute session, the psychiatrist, whom Marine and I referred to by his first name, would feature heavily in our conversations over the next thirteen years. Bernard, a dead ringer for Paul Auster and a calm, reserved, intellectual type, had an ethereal air about him and a distant attitude that made me feel it was safe to talk to him. By the end of our first meeting, it was settled: twice a week, Monday and Thursday. Six o'clock in the evening. We shook hands. The deal was sealed. Our regular meetings helped me keep my head above water. Session by session, question by question, one interjection after the next, my depressive tendencies, frenzied exercising and methodical, controlled eating patterns were slowly picked apart. But nothing could quell the anger and hatred I felt for my father. Nor could I shake those romantic fantasies.

I'd been drifting for so long, several times a day, between reality and my imaginary love affair. After the initial excitement, after the solitary fervour that had come over me, much to my astonishment, in that Paris hotel room, I had been suppressing my feelings assiduously. One day, when I felt his eyes on me during a meeting, waiting for my answer to a colleague's question, I gulped loudly, perturbed by his body only inches away from mine. I was certain my throat had betrayed my attraction to him, that he'd sensed my nervousness. When the meeting was over, I set to work on shuffling my projects around, trading any clients Paul was supervising with my colleagues' clients, even if they were more challenging. All it took was a bit of subtle insistence on my part, and Paul's father-in-law, who had taken a shine to me, took me off all the contracts we worked on regularly together. I had to do it. I was practically at the point of throwing myself at him, laughing like a fool at the slightest thing he said, twisting a strand of hair around my finger every time he spoke. I hoped distance would still my heart, stop it from racing the way it did in his presence. A modern-day Madame Bovary. It was ridiculous. Losing control was not an option.

He finally cornered me one day while I was standing in the office kitchen, drinking a coffee.

'It's a shame. I liked working with you.'

That was all he said.

I decided to imitate Charlotte, who had at least taught me something useful, and went into diva mode. Head tilted to the side, nose in the air, I answered him in a grotesque tone: 'I'm bored, Paul. I need a change of scene. And besides, it's better this way. For everyone.'

By some strange coincidence, I bumped into Charlotte a few days later. It was at a flashy soirée organized by a luxury brand and I had no choice but to attend.

Watching her surreptitiously, I saw she was as beguiling as ever. With years of hindsight, I've come to understand how she lures people in with her pompous, hypocritical ways. It's all in the way she looks, her airs and graces, that pout she's perfected, the way she has of making people feel they're special. She was even more fake than I remembered: we weren't even close to forty and there were already tell-tale signs of facial surgery and Botox. Too much perfume, too much gesticulating, too much pantomime, too much bullshit. She wins men over by laughing too hard at their jokes, compliments women, speaks in saccharine tones.

I caught snippets from the sidelines. She knew what she was doing. I might have found it amusing if I weren't already familiar with her shallow, seductive tricks. I had no sympathy for her because she's not stupid. She could have, should have put her intelligence to better use. She could have learned Arabic or Chinese or whatever else, rather than employing that sterile vernacular of seduction to take advantage of people. When our eyes met, she didn't even blink before she started sizing me up. No rush of tenderness, no trace of friendship remained of the years we had spent as a couple. I felt only bitterness and remorse. She came over and filled the awkward silence with her ranting. She was a psychologist now. 'But I can't work. It's impossible with Laurent being so busy, we're always on the go.' Laurent, a well-known businessman, had caused a stir when he had left the mother of his children, a woman who wasn't as pretty but who was much more honest than the manipulator standing before me. The split, followed by his marriage to Charlotte, had made the headlines several times. Laurent had the kind of charm typical of men in their forties, bolstered by professional recognition. The type of man who probably hadn't been much to look at in his youth, who'd had to perfect his sense of humour or some other talent while the good-looking guys got by on their appearance alone. He'd worked tirelessly, studying and networking to get ahead. A career, a reputation and a semblance of power were enough to make people forget his protruding ears. His puny build, once a cause of great shame, was now considered enviably slim. Laurent was a carbon copy of his father, Charlotte a clone of her mother. It didn't take a crystal ball to predict the future of their relationship. 'My dad's had a child who's younger than my own!' she told me. 'My mum looks like something out of Madame Tussauds.' Frankly, I'm astounded a psychologist can't see the blindingly obvious.

You should have gone for an even older model, you poor thing, I thought, adding: In ten years' time, you'll be on your own. Simply a bitch. I didn't need anything else on my conscience, which was already far from spotless. So I kept my mouth shut.

She was pathetic. She told me she was writing ('non-fiction, of course, the novel form is so banal nowadays'), lived in a chateau, and had a maid from India, who swam in the pool when she was away. ('Can you imagine? I fired the little witch.')

It was no longer a question of differences in opinion, education or culture. She was the embodiment of everything I loathed. Disregarding the usual etiquette for this kind of flashy event, she cut straight to the point as we moved into the gardens of the Hôtel Beau-Rivage.

'It's easier to pull the wool over men's eyes. It's true. I live a more comfortable life now. But you know…' She leaned towards me in a lewd, ridiculous motion. 'Of everyone I've ever had, Jeanne, you're my favourite.'

I don't know whether she's highly intuitive or just a bitch. I don't remember telling her about the sucker punch my sister dealt me that day: *I was his favourite*. Surely not. It had to be a coincidence. My confidence had grown over the years. I looked at her standing there in her black sheath dress, all muscle and swollen lips. I thought of Marine, who would chuck on any old thing in the morning, and her limitless sincerity and empathy. I thought of Paul and his endearingly kind nature. And I told myself I'd dodged a bullet by leaving her.

'I'm not sure what you're trying to imply, Charlotte, but it doesn't sound particularly nice.'

She took a quick glance around her then lowered her voice. 'You're still my favourite, Jeanne. Even though you hit me.'

We were a wretched pair. It was as though her presence released the cruelty in me. As though the shadow of my father were buried within me still. There was only one thing I wanted to do. Hit her.

11

I go there on Sundays. The day my father goes out on his jaunts. I drive on the way there to calm my mind. On the way back, I sit in monastic silence on the passenger side, face turned towards the window. With Marine, I don't have to spill my guts all over the dashboard. With Marine, I don't have to do anything. She takes the time to listen, she's never impatient or insistent, she asks only gentle questions. Once, when I told her how much I admired her ability to be so open with people without judging them, even hard and cynical people like me, she stopped me mid-sentence: 'It doesn't cost me anything.'

Mum is always there waiting for us, trying to hide her excitement. Her joy. We talk about everything and nothing. The conversation doesn't flow naturally. She never complains, she avoids mentioning my father. I tell her about my weekend in Turin or my dips in the lake, without giving too many details. She asks me to stop bringing her gifts. 'You need a scarf, Mum, it's getting cold. Don't you like the gloves?' 'It's not that...' She never talks about my father's jealousy, the scenes he makes after we leave. We always sit in the kitchen, which she spends hours sprucing up to make it look presentable.

One Sunday, I see my father's clapped-out car is parked under the walnut tree. My mother, who always takes great care to look good for our arrival, is standing on the doorstep, her hair completely dishevelled. She's wearing the smile she puts on when she's telling a lie or fighting back tears. 'In you come, I've baked something for you.' Apple pie, as always.

Marine didn't spend all those years behind closed doors with him. She doesn't know what's coming. But I know that from this point, every word, every gesture must be sugar-coated. Like a volcano about to erupt, the lava will come gushing forth. No one can say when, but the magma will overflow, taking with it our thoughts, our rationality, leaving only fear in its wake. So all we can do is try to delay the inevitable, avoid adding fuel to the fire. And yet we know it's coming. It could be anything or nothing, the rain or the sun, the cake or the coffee. Everything is a pretext for violence. I spent years trying to dissect those scenes. What if I hadn't said that? What if Mum hadn't put the cheese down there? Would it still have happened? Thanks to my sessions with Bernard, I know now that no amount of kindness, no precautions we take can deflect the wave.

He stands there in front of the table. It's the first time I've seen him in years. I didn't even come to see them at Christmas. He's drunk. His shirt is open, exposing his fat stomach.

'Here they are, the three little pigs.'

Every word and gesture becomes irrational, and yet you have to get through whatever comes next, no matter what. You will have to endure every moment and remember it afterwards, pick up each shard of glass from the floor, hands trembling, mop up the coffee splattered everywhere, keep yourself busy, try to still your heart. It's like watching a famous scene from a film and acting it out at the same time. You're in the frame, but everything's disjointed.

'Hello, Louis. How are you?' Marine automatically puts on her professional tone, the one I've heard her use for the families she works with when they call her in an emergency.

'Shut your mouth, you little dyke.'

You have to have known that kind of violence, the vulgarity that goes with it, to understand: there's no sense of reality to cling to from this point on. It all happens so quickly. There's no reason behind it. There's no context, no link between one word and the next. It's surreal. Sometimes, when I'm with a client, I find myself thinking: What would happen if I threw my glass of water in his face? I play out the scene in my head, the man jumping to his feet, yelling, clutching at his soaking wet shirt, mouth agape. But no one would dare. It just wouldn't happen. Except him, and others like him who live their lives with rage as their compass. A man once grabbed Marine by the throat after his children were placed in a shelter. She was able to reason with him. She could even sympathize. My father's rage, on the other hand, is impossible to reason with, because there's nothing to justify his actions.

We pretend to carry on talking among ourselves. Mum brings out the pie. When our eyes meet, I can tell she knows it too. We're not getting out of this one.

'Why do you have to come here? Just to piss everyone off? Why don't you just stay in Lausanne with your little whore instead of swanning around here? You're a disgrace to the family.'

He's speaking loudly, he's red in the face, he keeps clenching and unclenching his fists, chest puffed out, shoulders back to make himself look impressive. I'm scared, I'm so scared. I lower my head. Then I think back to those words I dared to say to him as a child. As a child, when my body was a fortress. Now I'm an adult, I'm much more vulnerable.

It all happens fast. Even though I know what he's capable of, it still manages to shock me. I let out a scream despite myself. He grabs me by the shoulder and I find myself pinned to the wall, one of his hands around my throat. His forehead is pressed up against mine as he squeezes, mouthing: 'You dirty whore.' Spittle lands in my eye. I'm frozen. It doesn't even occur to me to defend myself, to knee him in the balls, wrench myself from his grip. I'm a runner and a swimmer. I may be no match for his strength, but I'm strong. Yet I stand there stupidly, paralysed, eyes wide with terror. I'm petrified.

Marine is behind him. She may be shorter than me, but she's a long-distance runner. She grabs his shirt and tugs. She tries to make him loosen the hand that's choking me. My mother stands there with her hands over her mouth, too stunned to intervene. Finally, he eases his grip. Everything else is a blur. I try to collect myself. I hold my hand up to my throat. I hear Marine giving him a piece of her mind without raising her voice. He lowers his, ever so slightly. He walks over to the sideboard and in one fell swoop mows down the bouquet of wild anemones we brought.

'I just got fired. Those bastards fired me, for fuck's sake. Three years to go until retirement and they fire me. Bunch of fucking arseholes.'

'Are they giving you an early retirement package?' Marine ventures, softly.

'I don't care about those fucking big shots and their big words.'

He's still shouting.

Marine has done the unthinkable. She's made him verbalize what's making him angry, something we were never able to do. All three of us had fallen too deep into the cavernous cesspit he'd created. I think I see a twinge of shame in his eyes as he looks at me. But no. He gets up to leave.

The whole incident only lasted a few minutes, but it was enough to open the wounds. It had taken so many years, so many miles, so many hours of therapy and talking with Marine to try and alleviate some of the pain. But all I'd managed to do was temporarily numb it. A few minutes was all it took for me to fall back in. For the anguish to return at the thought of leaving my mother with him.

I begged her to come with us: 'Just a few days, please. A little holiday. Please, Mum. I'm begging you. Come with us. You can't stay here. Please. We can see each other without him being around. I'm too scared to leave you here, I'm scared that one of these days he's going to kill you.'

'I can't.'

'Of course you can. What are you afraid of? What's the worst that can happen? Please. Does he hit you? Does he push you around? What does he do?'

'No, it's fine. He just shouts, and I leave him to it. I don't say a word. At some point he just stops.'

But I know it goes on for hours. I've seen the way he paces around her while she's sitting in her armchair. I know.

His car had disappeared from under the walnut tree. I hugged my mother tight in my arms. I clung to her, crying, my chest engorged with grief. We left. As if nothing had happened. As if everything were normal. When nothing was normal at all.

I never got used to the violence. What's worse, when it stopped, I was plunged into a deep despair. It felt like having boiling hot oil poured over wounds that had never healed. For days, I remained mute, dazed, my morale devastated. One incident was all it took for those wounds to reopen. Like it happened only yesterday: my childhood, my sister. Like falling down a hole, slipping in with nothing to cling to, like having your heart spill out over your jumper, being startled by every little noise.

Marine is all patience, gentle coaxing, tender words and protective silences. Bernard listens attentively, his brow furrowed. For the first time, he suggests anti-anxiety medication. I refuse. I'm working on autopilot, late into the night.

I'm not at all with it. I'm constantly wearing a mask. Marine insists on me going to the mountains or the sea, either alone or with her. The only glimmer of light is Paul. Knowing he's in his office, not far from my own, soothes my sadness. But I can't talk to him. We're never together. I barely see him any more since putting a distance between us, since getting promoted. I'm free, independent, smart, athletic, strong, educated, gay. Some people even tell me I'm brilliant. But I'm shattered on the inside, unable to pick myself up after the incident. Paul may not know it, but he helps me survive by simply being there. I feel guilty for having left my mother with that monster, guilty for betraying Marine, guilty for thinking of Paul. I'm going under.

At some point I realize I'm drinking every night. I go from drinking a glass each evening to finishing a whole bottle. I'm aggressive towards my colleagues, slow cashiers, people who skip the queue in the supermarket. Other people's trite problems annoy me, I become bitter, I get angry at friends over nothing. Bernard insists on signing me off work: 'You're hardly sleeping. You're going to explode.' I get a phone call from Marine. She's seriously worried about me. 'You need medication.' I'm struggling. It lasts for weeks. Hold on, I tell myself. Just hold on.

A Parisian client who has become a friend calls me about some upcoming launches. We have to meet up. In Lausanne this time. She has a vague idea about my tormented childhood, she can sense my despair. The distance helps me let go. I lock myself in the office and burst into tears. It's my father. I keep replaying it all in my head; I feel like I'm stuck in a really dark place, like a black night that never ends. When I stop to take a breath my whole childhood plays out before my eyes. The only thing keeping me going is work, thank God I have that, otherwise... Within minutes, she's concocted a plan: 'Cancale. You can take my house. Give yourself a breather. Plus, you love to swim. I know it's not going to solve the root of the problem. But it'll give you a bit of a boost.'

'Yes,' I say. Half-heartedly. But she and I both know I'm not going on a mini break to Brittany to perk myself up.

12

He shuts the door and asks me cautiously if everything is OK.

I've been holding back my feelings for years now. I'd contented myself with the romantic and erotic dreams of him. I learned to temper the desire when it became too intense. I felt huge bursts of tenderness towards him, a lump rising in my throat and a smile spreading across my face the second I heard him talking and joking in the corridor. I put a lid on my emotions. The love Marine and I shared was tender and serene. That girl was like a ray of sunshine. She made everything poetic. She was easy-going, she took me to parties and introduced me to new friends. She always had room in her heart, always made life spontaneous. She once took a homeless person in for a while, always gave money to people in the streets. Always. 'If I have anything, I always give it.' I admired her for her endless, uncalculating empathy. 'It's nothing,' she would say. 'That's just the way I am.' And still Paul refused to budge from my thoughts, no matter how many years went by, no matter how fierce and desperate my attempts to get him out of my head and my heart.

And now he's sitting there right in front of me. Giving me a strange look. 'What's going on, Jeanne?'

'Nothing. Why? Have I done something wrong?'

'No, you've done everything right. But something doesn't seem quite right with you.'

A finger to my lips, I look at him and listen, cold on the outside, petrified on the inside. I don't even know how I've found myself alone in a room with him. I'd been feeling quietly smug, congratulating myself for successfully keeping this man out of my mind. But right now, I'm not doing a great job of it.

'Listen, Jeanne. I...' He leans forward, looking at the floor, and runs his hand through his hair. He places his elbows on the armrests and rests his chin in his palms. He looks odd, uncomfortable.

'Are you firing me, Paul?' Why else would he have called me in?

'No. I'm not firing you. Of course not. I can see you haven't been doing well lately. I mean... I don't know. What's wrong? Is it work?'

'No, it's nothing to do with work. It's complicated. A family thing. I'm sorry if my work has been suffering.'

'That's not what I'm saying! I just... I can just tell you're not all right. And it makes me sad to see it. I...' He's stammering, struggling to find the words.

'Just say it, Paul. I don't understand what you're trying

to tell me. I'm sorry if my work is suffering. I'll make up for it, I promise.'

'I… All right then. Just know you mean a lot to me.'

I sense the awkwardness, but also the tenderness. I can feel it there between us from across the table, though he is usually so eloquent when it comes to public speaking. I've tried to convince myself it isn't genuine, that he tries to appear humble and down to earth to casually seduce employees and clients. But now that eloquence has vanished. My resolve to keep my distance vanishes now he's here in front of me. We look at each other in silence.

'There are some things that can't be said. Not at work. You… I… We have this thing. I can't explain it, because it's not rational. There's a connection. I mean, I feel a connection between us. I don't know what it is, but what I do know is that you're not OK, and I can't bear to see you like that. I want you to know that I'm here if you need me.'

My head is spinning. My brain can't keep up with what's happening. I could spill my guts right here, on the table between us, tell him about the thoughts that inhabit me, tell him that I'm practically leading a double life. I could find the courage to speak, spit it out, confess my unspoken love, expunge my feelings. Words may not always speak the truth, but we all know they can alter reality. Completely. And there's no going back. Before and after. Before, comfort. After, a whirlwind. And so we lock away the feelings in our stomachs, we seal the lips that yearn to speak, we clamp them tight between our teeth to keep those fools from talking. Would I be stupid enough to take the bait, this first intimation of his feelings, and throw myself at him, my feet, my belly, my whole flesh and heart? Revel in my own interpretation of a few stock phrases after years of fantasizing? *You mean a lot to me*. It's too much and not enough. Would I be so stupid as to make a fool of myself, risk rejection, all for a few words? Of course not. I've always held my morals high like a banner, brandishing them in every discussion. I've always been repulsed by tales of deception, despised anyone too cowardly to make a decision. I wasn't a fool, but I was fooling myself. Every day. It's not infidelity if it's only a fantasy, I'd told myself.

'Thank you, that's kind of you. If I need to talk, I know where to find you. It's not all fun and games right now, but I have people I can talk to.'

Paul, level-headed as always, nodded and forced a smile.

That smile took me back to a night a few years ago, when I was having a drink in a bistro with Marine and some friends. We were busy debating some topic or other when I saw him leaning against the bar talking to another man. I didn't recognize him at first. He was wearing jeans and a jumper; at work he was always in a suit. He was even more stunning like that. One of the girls in the group turned to me and said: 'Never thought I'd see you checking a guy out!' Thank God the lighting was dim, because my cheeks were on fire. 'That's Paul. Over there at the bar.' They all knew him by name, but no one had ever met him. The whole table turned to look at him at once. He saw us, nodded, then raised his glass and smiled at me. Marine said: 'Christ!

What a smile.' What a smile indeed. Even in an awkward situation like this.

'Is that all you have to say? I understand you're not doing well. But that's no reason to be so cold. You know me by now, you know I'm not one to talk. At least not about personal things. That's fair to say, isn't it? I feel like an idiot. But I stand by what I said. That's all I have to say.' As he leaves my office, disappointed with the convincing wall of coldness I've built up, he adds: 'Almost all.'

I take a piece of paper and a pencil and start writing. Without stopping, without thinking.

I love you, Paul, and I don't know what to do with that love. It's all I think about from the moment I get up. The moment I open my eyes, it's already there, lurking. Nobody else can see it. I feel it when I'm getting ready, when I take a cold shower, when I put a few spoonfuls of the coffee I got from a little shop in Val d'Aosta in my moka pot. It ebbs and flows, but it's always there. It's a gentle breeze, it's a train ride, it's the water in the lake, grey or blue or green, rippling or still, it's a blissful song, it's a voice I hear on the radio. It's alive; sometimes I think it's following me. I don't know a thing about you. Which side of the bed do you sleep on? Do you shower in the morning or at night, do you jump in and out or do you take your time? Is the water lukewarm or scalding hot? Do you snore? What do you read and where? Do you like oysters? Does chocolate turn your stomach like it does mine? Are your moans loud or soft? Do you have any siblings? Older or younger? Do you ever cry? Why? I know nothing, nothing, nothing about you. And yet we have this invisible connection. I thought it was a figment of my imagination, something that only existed in dreams. Not a day goes by when you're not there, a disturbing presence.

You don't know a thing about me, either. You don't know where I'm from. I'm haunted, tarnished by my past howling at me all through the night, rearing its head when I least expect it. All it takes is the sound of shouting, a plate being broken, a ruckus in the street, and all the fear and hatred resurface. What you see of me, what I show you, is the part of me I've tamed. I've sucked the lifeblood out of the women I've known, I wallow in my father's violence when I should be growing up. You would be ashamed on my behalf if you knew the truth. I subsist on my own anger. It's how I survive. Little did I know that loving you, even from a distance, would show me the meaning of tenderness. And all you had to do was exist. I'm afraid of throwing away all my efforts to stay afloat for a love I've romanticized too much for it to ever be real. I'm afraid of letting myself love you completely. I'm afraid of falling if I let down the barriers that separate us. I have to get away from you, Paul. It's better this way.

I saved myself six months of sessions with Bernard in one single draft, spewed out onto the page without a second thought. I realized how trapped I was in my hatred, how resistant I was to change, constantly going over the same memories in my mind. I was unable to forgive. Other people have suffered too. They move on. Marine lost her father as a child and her mother, too young to be alone, worked herself to the bone. She doesn't blame anyone. I just keep stagnating. Marine, Marine, sunshine of my life. If she knew, would she leave me? My silence protected us both. I put away the letter in my desk.

13

With each stroke, the water splits in two. Crawl. One, two. Breathe. Repeat. Crawl. One, two. Air. I need to clear my head. I'm still numb from our talk. I don't feel shock or joy or comfort in anything. Life keeps on sneaking up on me from behind, appropriating desires that were never supposed to become a reality, taking them into its own hands. This unexpected turn has left me gasping for air, but life forges on with its impeccable mechanics whether I like it or not. The weather is mild, June has made itself at home, the water is clear, there's nothing for it but to dive in. And burn that piece of paper with my bumbling, gushy scribbles, my declaration of love.

I yearned to be capable of lightness, to be flexible instead of rigid. I didn't want to throttle my feelings and desires. I wanted to stroke his cheek with the tips of my fingers, to gaze at him intensely, to skim the contours of his skin with my nose, a hint of a smile on my lips as I dared to press them to the corner of his. I wanted his hand to venture towards my face, the other tightening its grip around my back, as our bodies brushed against one another, as we sought each other out, as I finally breathed in his scent, felt the tip of his tongue. How many hundreds of times have I replayed the scene in my head? How many hundreds of times have I told myself Marine deserves better, that I'm more than just some hare-brained woman with vapid fantasies about love? At no point did I see that my adoration for Paul was an attempt to seek out a man who would never hurt me.

Marine prided herself in asking for loyalty rather than fidelity. I was faithful, but I couldn't say I was loyal. In the bracing water, the weight of my body lifted, I can see clearly. I swim breaststroke back to the shore, praying to the same God I gave up on before the age of ten, imploring Him to watch over Marine.

I could pick up my life where I left off a few hours ago. Forget about Paul and his clumsy words that had devastated the pitiful foundations I had built for myself. Instead, I go back to the office, deserted at this hour, and slip my letter into an envelope: the first love letter I've ever written. I put it in his locker.

When I walk into the flat, shouting 'hello' as always, I feel the breeze coming in through the living room window that opens onto the balcony and its clear view of the lake. That was the main reason we chose to rent the flat on Boulevard de Grancy, though it was a little large for just the two of us. Then I see her standing straight as a ramrod in the hallway leading to each of the rooms, lips pursed, eyes round, brow furrowed.

'It's your mum.' I see the duffel bag out of the corner of my eye. I understand without her telling me that we have to leave for Valais. She takes me in her arms and says: 'I'm sorry.' For what? I don't hear her, don't understand. It must be my father, maybe an illness. What is she talking about, an accident? It's only as we're driving up through Montreux, absorbed by the unwavering majesty of Lake Geneva, that I finally hear, finally grasp what Marine has been trying to tell me since we left. It's as though a veil muffling the sounds has been lifted. Car crash. Another driver overtaking. Collision. Head-on. Fatal.

Once again, everything switches to autopilot when death is pronounced. The hard facts. The tightening of the solar plexus, keeping the pain locked inside when the heart wants to brim over. The funeral home, choosing an outfit, choosing a photograph for the obituary in *Le Nouvelliste*, deciding on a bistro so people can gorge themselves on rye bread, cured meat and alpine cheese as though they haven't eaten in days. Being surrounded by strangers, old relatives you have the misfortune of sharing blood with, waiting for it all to be over so you can be alone. Valaisian rituals are hard, heavy, ancient, but they're also required by tradition. First there's the vigil in the chapel, where the family, choked with grief, remains nailed to the bench as the whole village files by in a mournful procession. Now and then, a voice punctuates the silence to recite the rosary – an Our Father here, a few Hail Marys there – before the supplicant implores an endless list of saints: 'Pray for us.' Mourning the dead is a primitive tradition. Whether it provides relief, I can't say. But it helps us to get through death in the public eye. In Italy, they have professional mourners. In Valais, women spontaneously recite prayers or the rosary in monotonous tones, their wooden or plastic beads clicking against one another. And then there's the rest, all of it unbearable, interminable. The social obligations do nothing to help heal. But they do compel people to momentarily forge a kind of twisted affinity among themselves. My mother didn't work, my father was the guy nobody wanted anything to do with, and despite all that: the crowd. I'm sitting in the front row next to my father, who won't stop crying. He's a disgrace. He never had an ounce of dignity. And yet dignity is what kept my mother going. She'd starch all the clothes, no matter how old, she kept her hair and nails tidy, polished away every scratch that appeared on our shoes. Once, over the phone, she confessed to having tried alcohol: 'I liked the feeling of numbness. It seemed to muffle your father's screaming, make the words seem less vulgar. It didn't sound quite so loud when he was shouting. It didn't hurt quite as much when he called me a dirty whore. But I didn't want to bring shame on the family. I stopped to preserve what little dignity I had.'

Two days before the burial, as I was looking in her wooden wardrobe to choose the last dress she'd ever wear – she never wore trousers – a memory of an Easter morning came to me. The whole village was gathered ceremoniously for High Mass. But it wasn't enough to simply turn up and celebrate the resurrection of Christ. You also had to show off your outfit for spring, or 'spring clothes' as we called them, which, from that week on, would also become your Sunday best. Everyone in the village would be there to see you in your new get-up and your shiny shoes, to find out just how much money you had. Originally, no doubt, it was a question of courtesy, of presenting one's best self at the feet of the Lord. There were all types: discreet, flashy, humble, well off. And all of them participated in the masquerade. My father, holder of the purse strings and ever the selfish, shifty penny-pincher, drew out a few hundred-franc notes specially for the occasion so my mother could buy nice clothes for herself and for the rest of us. He would also be the judge of whether we looked shabby. But there weren't any clothes for ten francs hanging there on the rack, waiting for us. Dressing up came at a cost. Mum had to find a way to cobble our three outfits together. When we were little, she'd knit little cardigans for my sister and me from cheap wool she'd managed to find at Uniprix. But that year, when I must have been about nine, my father's sister took her to one of the few clothing shops in our town. Emma, already a little trendsetter, was delighted. I still remember the exact layout of that shop, where the beau monde went for their clothes, and the owner, a sour, unpleasant woman. My sister was bouncing all over the place in a yellow jumper with lions on the front and a matching pair of checked trousers. You couldn't take your eyes off her with her bright yellow outfit and golden mane of hair, her body already exultantly feminine. My mother chose a simple black dress with little white flowers that was on sale and would need to be altered because it was too long for her five-foot-tall frame. I only liked wearing trousers and dreamed of owning a pair of trainers but, swept up in all the joy, I picked out a navy-blue, pleated skirt that went down to just below the knee. Everyone set to work finding me a blouse. 'You'll need patent shoes and white stockings,' the saleswoman advised me. It was like a Japanese school uniform; I had never seen anything so beautiful. I was absorbed by my own reflection in the mirror. It wasn't me but somebody else full of poise. Elegance, almost.

'That's not the fashion, Jeanne. Honestly, you can't go out looking like that,' my sister lectured.

I was mesmerized. I couldn't speak. Standing there in that skirt, I felt myself transcending the conditions my father imposed on us. Without knowing why, my mother sensed that I had fallen in love with this little outfit, which was far beyond our means. She nodded, stroking my hair. An interlude of discreet whispers ensued between the saleswoman, who was a friend of my aunt, while the latter started digging in her purse. My mother was clearly embarrassed, but also determined to make my wish come true. I had no idea how much those pieces of fabric cost – 'A fortune!' my mother told me, years later. I could sense her worry. That evening she was pacing up and down in the kitchen by herself. The next day, when I got home from school, she told me we had to return the little skirt. 'No, no, no…' I cried. 'Please, Mum…' But she stood her ground. My aunt came to pick us up. We had to wait for the shop to close to return the purchase in secret with the help of the nice blonde lady who worked there. I overheard her saying: 'My boss can be very mean. She mustn't find out about this.' Swiftly, she gave my aunt her money back. 'We aren't part of that world,' my mother said as we were leaving. 'We won't be going back.' Years later, I went to a department store in Geneva with Charlotte and saw a pleated skirt almost identical to the one from my memory. Charlotte was crying with laughter. 'You look like a nun! That's not you at all.' I didn't expect her to understand. I bought it. Once again it was too expensive, but I couldn't pass up on the opportunity to recreate a childhood memory. I still have it. I rarely ever wear it. But of all the clothes I own, it's my favourite.

When I opened the mothball-infested double wardrobe, I spotted the black-and-white dress she'd bought more than twenty-five years ago. She still had it. It had barely been worn. Hands trembling, I spread it out on my parents' bed – they had shared a marital bed all their lives. I imagined her there every night over the decades, praying to God and all the saints for him not to touch her. As I ran my fingers along the material, tears came streaming down my cheeks, one after the other. I remembered her in that dress, still young but dressed like a grandmother. I remembered how much she wanted to make me happy that Easter. How brave she was, how much she wanted to spoil me, how her humble dream was shattered. She knew she had to protect me from him; she knew I would have got a thrashing and so would she. What kind of a life is that? How many years of fear and loneliness? How many years of waiting for me? Of mourning her daughter's suicide? Almost as much as I blamed my father, I blamed her for not leaving him, for not running away. It was her duty, she said, or sometimes, on her darkest days, her 'fate'. She was resigned to it. She respected the laws of marriage and feared the villagers' judgement even more. The Valaisian motto may as well be *Just grin and bear it*. There were aspects of that tenacious Valaisian character I could see in myself. My tough nature was shaped as much by my father as it had been by Valais: its unforgiving geography and elements, the mountains that isolated us from the rest of the world, those vertical black-and-grey rock faces. I was finally able to see and appreciate a more endearing side to where I came from. But I couldn't accept how much of a drastic sacrifice my mother had made.

Not long before she died, as she was wrapping up a piece of aged cheese for Marine and me, I remember saying to her: 'Mum, please come to Lausanne. We have a room for you. We'll find you a flat. You can get a divorce. Please. Please come! There's nothing keeping you here.'

'I'm not unhappy. Not in the slightest.'

'What are you doing with your life? Waiting around here for the next beating?'

'He doesn't beat me like he used to. He's getting tired. He's getting old. Emma's death calmed him down.'

'Stop! I'm not talking about Emma, I'm talking about you. What are you doing with your life, Mum? Answer the question. This place is completely hopeless. It's claustrophobic.'

'That's only how you see it. My life is my life. It's not for you to judge. I might not have done great things. But I have my ways. And I have my dreams.'

'What are your dreams? What do you dream of, Mum?'

'You wouldn't understand. I have my life, which you clearly despise, and I have my dreams. That's enough for me.'

'I don't despise your life, Mum. I despise him.'

'You're not a little girl any more. You shouldn't be day-dreaming at your age. Get your head out of the clouds, Jeanne.'

14

Marine and I kept things dignified, as Mum would have wanted. We were impervious to the whispers of onlookers waiting in the pews, some discreetly turning their heads to watch us as we walked up the aisle of the church. I silently said my last goodbyes and held back the grief quietly thrumming inside me. It was all I could do not to let it out in one great roar.

I recognized Paul by the back of his neck. He was sitting in a pew with a handful of my friends. His messy hair clashed with the sober suit he'd put on for the occasion. I was ashamed to be thinking about him right then.

Our village choir is made up of only men. Singers said to be known far and wide. The powerful, masterful voices of those men brought a reverent solemnity to the burial. It was beautiful. My mother deserved that unpretentious beauty. I didn't know those men, towering over everyone from the organ above, 'up in the pipes', as they say. And yet that day they made my grief more bearable. I don't remember the songs, the tunes or the sermons. All I remember is the ray of sunlight shining through the stained-glass windows onto the nave. I lifted my head to look and imagined Mum looking down with a smile, no longer physically there but still alive in my heart. I was up in the clouds, too, swaddled in sedatives. Delphine, a friend of mine who owns a holiday chalet in Vercorin, let us stay with her for a few days. She gave me the sedatives, saying: 'They'll help you get through.' I wasn't really there, but at least I didn't have to struggle against the tide of grief – the chemicals did that for me.

I was surprised and saddened to see Dr Fauchère there. He slowed down when he passed our pew. He didn't stop for the customary handshake.

'Look who it is. That arsehole!'

The appearance of Dr Fauchère immediately put a stop to my father's tears. Even at his wife's funeral, sitting at the foot of her coffin, he had to be rude.

I avoided the perfunctory greetings. I didn't owe anyone anything. I wasn't avoiding anyone out of contempt. I just wanted to be alone. The only company I could tolerate over those few days was that of Marine and Delphine, who were considerate and discreet. I didn't give a damn about the social obligations, the handshakes, the fakeness, the awkward hugs. Time hadn't weathered this place in the slightest since the last time I had come and caused a scene. The memory was so fresh in my mind, it was like I was burying not only my mother but also Emma for the second time. The hearse left slowly, ceremoniously, a moment I never wanted to end. It occurred to me there, at the bottom of the steps, that there weren't many of us left. Only a small bunch of our affectionless little family remained. The rest of the gawkers had had the decency to leave us alone with our grief.

Mechanically, I carried out each movement, without thinking, copying Marine when I didn't know what to do. 'We'll do things the way you want,' she said. 'You don't owe anybody anything.' Friends had come. It would have been enough simply to know they were there. But they came over to see me. I don't remember now which of them patted me on the shoulder, which of them hugged me a little tighter than usual. Looking back on those moments makes the grim ordeal bearable, even long after it's over. Though they came from different places, different cities, different cantons, everyone respected the funeral protocol of my home. Their gestures, their attire, their expressions. Their presence. Delphine was waiting for us in the car park behind the church so we could escape the traditional banquet. It was practically deserted. Marine stroked my hunched back as we walked towards the car.

'Jeanne.'

I knew that voice. He was alone. We stopped. Marine, intuitive and understanding as ever, whispered, 'I'll wait for you in the car.'

Only then did he come over. My jaw was aching from clenching my teeth. Only then did I rest my forehead against his shoulder. Only then did he wrap his arms around me. Only then did he interlace his hands behind my back.

Only then did I cry, keeping him at a distance, my bent elbows pressed against my chest. Only then did I pull away and look at him.

15

We left for Lausanne the next day. My boss called to offer his condolences and apologize for not being there on the day of the funeral. He told me in a fatherly way to take all the time I needed before coming back: an order, not a suggestion, he added. I drifted between the lake and my bed, my bed and the lake. I avoided busy times; it was an extraordinarily hot July that year. I couldn't sleep, I tossed and turned all night in cold sweats. By five in the morning, I'd already be getting out of the lake. I wasn't swimming my usual kilometre of crawl, letting the water wash over me below the smooth surface of the lake between breaths. The only time of the day I felt alive was when my head was submerged in that cool morning water. When I wasn't in the lake, I hid myself away. I never spoke. I never cried in front of anyone else. But violent fits of tears took hold of me when I was least expecting them. I would double over crying and curl myself up in a ball, hands clasped over my mouth. My lips were gnawed to pieces. Marine was perfect as ever.

She never showed any signs of impatience. She understood that this final bout of mourning had left me in bits. She would often tentatively suggest I make an appointment with Bernard now our regular sessions had come to an end. I built up a wall around myself. Paul called me several times. I didn't answer. I couldn't allow any joy to coexist with the pain, couldn't accept the guilt sweeping over me in waves.

One day, early in the morning, instead of swimming, I decide to take a walk by the lake. As I'm crossing the path, someone calls my name. It's Pascale, a journalist friend. She's the editor of one of the leading daily papers, but her dream is to captain a boat. 'And not just a small one! One of those big boats on Lake Geneva that leave a white foam behind them as they go. I'd give it all up to be able to do that,' she once told me as we were having a drink in her work cafeteria. She covers the several metres between us in a few long strides. I thank her for the affectionate note she sent me a few weeks earlier. To spare her the embarrassment that comes with every first meeting after a death, I ask her what she's doing up that early in the day.

'Are you working on a report?'

'No, no. I've just come back from my boat. I'm selling it. Someone's coming to look at it this evening, so I wanted to check it over before going to work.'

'You're not selling it, are you? You love that boat so much! You haven't had it long.'

'I've found an even better one.' She sighs. 'It's time for me to part with it. I don't have the money or space to keep it in the harbour.'

The boat is a sign. For the first time in weeks, I feel a sense of feverish excitement. I explain to her how exotic a boat feels to us mountain folks. Many a winter we've spent together splashing around in our swimming caps and wetsuits, frozen but invigorated every time we manage to tackle the icy water, even just for a few minutes. I've never mentioned my dream to her. It always felt pretentious and unattainable.

'How much do you want for it?'

'Don't you want to look at it first?'

'No, I trust you. It's not like you're going to fleece me.'

She had bought it for next to nothing. One of her father's clients desperately needed the money and let it go for a nominal fee. 'My dad's a mechanic, so he's fixed up the engine. I could get more for it, but as it's you, I'll sell it for the price I paid plus the repairs. I know it's silly, but it was my first boat and I'm attached to it. It would genuinely make me happy to know it's going to you.'

I get a rush of exhilaration.

'I'd like to keep it until October,' she says. 'That way you can try it. We'll go out together and I'll teach you. You'll have to get your licence, too. Let's speak about it later on the phone.'

'Promise you won't sell it to anyone else.'

'I promise.'

'It's a deal.'

The boat has softened the shell of despair surrounding me. I run back up the steep street, thanking all those saints

I became reacquainted with in the chapel where my mother's humble coffin was laid.

Her body had been propelled through the windscreen in the accident. Dismembered, probably. We hadn't been allowed to see her. When the undertaker said the coffin was sealed, and no, it could not be opened, I bent double in shock. One of my cousins grabbed me by the shoulders and dragged me outside. I cried out like an animal. It was an extremely intimate moment. There were only a few of us there. I screamed so much I fell to my knees, deathly pale. I cried until no sound came out, while this person, practically a stranger, comforted me uneasily but assuredly, by this point crying himself. I managed to return to the chapel with the help of Marine and my cousin, dazed and torn by that powerful, immeasurable grief. As soon as the chapel closed, Marine took me straight to Delphine's cottage and drugged me with lorazepam to help me calm down and sleep through to the next morning.

Once I knew that boat was at the port, a stone's throw away from my flat, once I'd seen photos of it, I was reborn. It didn't stop the lingering pain, the insomnia, the sobbing fits that would strike without warning. The mere smell of apple pie was still enough to leave me in bits. The sight of a weary woman clutching her bag on her knees with both hands would break my heart. But by its mere existence, the humble little boat had thrown me a rope, allowing me to extricate myself from the hellish downward spiral. It gave me an incredible boost, the strength I needed to gently pick myself back up again. And to reach out to Paul.

16

'It's me.'

'Jeanne!'

That was all.

We listened on the phone to the shy silence filled only by our breaths. I smiled for the second time in weeks. I hadn't seen him since the funeral.

'Jeanne…' He says it again. 'Where are you?'

'At home.'

I'd been feeling suffocated by Marine. And she sensed it. On a whim, she'd gone to join her brother, whom she adored and saw too little of, in a little commune in the south called Sallagriffon. She needed headspace after living with a silent, miserable, depressing zombie for all this time.

'Do you want to meet?'

'Yes.' My heart was sputtering so hard, I was convinced he'd hear it beating turbulently on the other end of the line. 'Are you sure?'

'Yes.'

When we had united in that silent duet after my mother's funeral, an unspoken confession was made. A language that didn't need words, that spoke on our behalf.

I'm reluctant to invite him to mine, where the footprints of my life with Marine mark the walls, the furniture, the cups and the pillowcases. But where else to go? A hotel? Too seedy. A restaurant? Too risky, and I barely eat a thing these days. I know it would be a despicable thing to do, inviting him into our home together. But I'm selfish, even if I have everything to lose. For a split second I think I'm losing my mind, that Paul is nothing more than a hallucination, a whim that's led me astray. What if the connection he claims to feel is nothing but a cheap line, a feeble illusion? Then I think back to that moment we shared, standing there outside the church, the way he trembled as he held me. The doubt vanishes. It's like the boat all over again, only much more powerful.

'Come over.'

When the doorbell rings, I stand there, leaning against the door frame. I take one last breath. I open the door. We look at each other. For a long time. Without blinking. He comes towards me. I step back. He closes the door. We stand there, millimetres apart. For a long time. With the tip of my finger, I trace a line from the bridge of his nose to the corner of his mouth. He takes care of the rest, placing his hand on the back of my neck, his lips on mine. Slowly, patiently, our mouths come together. There's no stopping from there. Our cheeks, our ears, every inch of skin, our eyes, our hands. Still standing in the doorway, we use our tongues to explore one another with a meticulous tenderness that goes on and on.

We smother each other with kisses, cling to one another a little too tightly. A tangle of jumpers, belts being unbuckled by trembling hands. Jeans falling limp around ankles like stringless puppets. His intoxicating smell fills me with tenderness. His bare skin and the faint smell of soap make my heart somersault and awaken every one of my senses. His flesh, my inquisitive tongue. A man's body. The first my curious palms have ever touched. Muscles not quite as tender as the ones belonging to the only two other bodies I know. Not a word passes our lips, only the sound of our moans, our gestures filling the space with a feverish urgency. Right there on the floor, on the grey hallway carpet, he savours my entire body with fervour and tenderness in equal measures. From my hair down to my toes, from my shoulder blades to my ankle bones. We explore every part of one another with our noses. Our bodies have been crying out for so long. Every dip and contour. He bites, I scratch, I swallow, he sighs, I nestle into his neck, he plays with my fingers, I close my eyes, he kisses them, I open them, he smiles. It's a choreography of instincts. Each of us responds to the ebb and flow of the other's movements. Moments after we explode in a surge of pleasure, sweating, jolting, shuddering, the endless kisses and embraces begin once again. We each affectionately whisper the other's name, lips brushing against temples. We relish each other with parted lips. It happens on a Friday in August.

I closed the door behind him on Saturday night and rested my head against it. On the other side, I heard him step into the lift.

The bed was still crumpled from our frenetic lovemaking. I swaddled myself in the sheets.

A traitor, but whole. And ready to live.

17

There were two of them. Two cruel, vicious neighbours. A toxic duo, brought together by the perverse pleasure they got from making younger kids suffer. There was no escaping them. Same school, same route. I often walked alone. My sister was part of a trio with two other girls. I dawdled along, collecting branches, leaves or flowers. I was still in nursery. They lured me in by telling me they'd found a rabbit in the school basement. It was grey, damp and completely dark, save for the snatches of light slipping from the long corridor through the cracks of the door.

They pushed me into a room on the right and one of them switched on a bare light bulb. 'In here,' they said. I crouched to look inside the wicker basket on the ground. As I bent over, one grabbed my head with his hands while the other lifted my dress, pulled down my knickers and started inserting pebbles, one by one, into my anus. Maybe six. Maybe ten. I screamed. 'Shut up.' There was a hand covering my mouth. 'Now get lost,' they said finally, sniggering.

Another time they forced me to climb into a large oil or petrol barrel that had been dumped by a lorry.

'Get in!'

'No, I don't want to.'

They kicked me to make me go faster. I complied. I had to. I climbed up on the concrete bricks leading up to the opening of the steel cylinder that had been laid out specially. I swung one leg over the rim, followed by the other. I tried to keep my balance as its edge sliced into my buttocks. I slid in. The barrel was much bigger than me. I was so small. I still remember everything. Their sardonic laughter as they ran off. The barrel was filled with nettles.

Yet another of their dirty tricks: I found them sitting on the low wall behind the metal waste containers. They lured me in by pretending to be friendly: 'Come and play with us!' I was so used to being rejected and mocked by them that I thought this time they really meant it. Delighted about the prospect of making friends, I sat down proudly beside them, my hands resting on my bare legs. It was summer and I was wearing shorts, my feet bare and dirty from frolicking about on the washed-out tarmac. 'Go over there,' they said, pointing to the containers.

'What for?'

'You'll see, it's amazing.'

I hesitated. They insisted. At the age of four or five, it was impossible to imagine any form of sadism other than my father's. How was I supposed to anticipate a devilish plot hatched by two kids barely older than I was?

'Take off your shoes.'

I obeyed them in the hope they would accept me. I stepped onto the steel plate. It was searing hot. Mercilessly hot.

They were long gone by the time my screams alerted a passer-by. The soles of my feet stuck to the metal like magnets, skin peeling away. I shrieked. I don't remember who took me home. I was only half-conscious. I remember my mother leaning over me, a grave expression on her face. The cold washcloth on my forehead. I was delirious. That's when my father came in.

'That fucking child will do anything to get noticed.'

On some primal, simplistic level, I concluded that men brought nothing but pain. It was not a physical, intellectual, or ideological choice so much as a firm, voluntary intention set on the cusp of adolescence. Yet perhaps my preference for women had not been as intentional as I'd imagined? Was it possible that my homosexuality had been a choice resulting from pain? The pain of being rejected by those I simply wanted to love me: my father and Doctor Fauchère. This promise I made to myself as a child was sustained by my father's relentless reign of terror and my immense disappointment in Dr Fauchère, whom I despised. Intuitively, in an attempt to protect myself, had I followed my survival instinct and gravitated towards the place where I assumed no one would harm me?

Paul was different. I wasn't terrified by his strong physique. Everything was light, joyful, simple, tender, passionate. His body felt as familiar to me as my own. He was gentle, innocent. The week Marine was away, we saw each other every night. I wanted to know everything about him: his childhood summers spent in Puglia; his family, who, from his descriptions, had a Valaisian humility about them. He only told me snippets about his wife. Yes, he had accepted the job, no, he had no regrets, that was just the way it was. Even if he wasn't happy about the situation, he was a happy person. He was warm, funny, a man of few words, words that came in fits and starts. His chest was smooth. His whole body moved whenever he laughed. He always brought food to cook and ate a lot. We sipped red wine on the balcony in the middle of the night. Over the course of those few days, I laughed at his childhood stories, his dreadful teenage antics. I cried when I told him stories about Mum. I recounted some of the horrors, he comforted me with caresses and consoling words. I thought back to the beginning of my relationship with Marine. My reverence for her humanity, her capacity to love unconditionally, was self-evident. I liked how she soothed my wounds with her words and kisses.

He had a gentle, magical power over me. Was it simply fraternal? What was I looking for? What did I want? I was lonely, yet unable to be alone. It was one hell of a mess.

I check my watch. Twelve kilometres; fifty-eight minutes and counting. I'm back on form.

18

After. After, life goes on. After the death of my mother. After those crazy, tender, foolish hours with Paul. I have to go on. Pretending. Lying. The feelings are at odds with one another. It's a merry-go-round of grief and love, values and treachery. Living in the solitude of secrecy, torn apart by opposing feelings.

Sometimes my anger is directed at Mum, the way she submitted to her husband and the silent, authoritarian injunctions of the village. Sometimes I miss her so much that the knot in my stomach rises into my throat. One afternoon, at the supermarket in Le Closelet, I bump into a girl from school. We haven't seen each other since then. Her face has barely changed, apart from having lost its fresh-faced plumpness and acquired a few furrows here and there. It's strange how, once you get over the shock of how much time has passed, irrevocably leaving its stigmata on the flesh, once you ask yourself where you know that face from, you still recognize a person. We hug each other. A formality.

After exchanging a few words, after the customary three kisses, we remember that we never were close. 'I'm sorry to hear about your mum.' *Mum.* Not *mother.* Perhaps it's the affection contained in the word, which feels incongruous standing in front of a Migros supermarket with a packet of rice and a lettuce tucked under my arm. Perhaps it's the banal, homely intimacy of the scene. Either way, I'm in floods of tears. Just like that. I apologize, she rubs my upper arm awkwardly in embarrassment, I immediately turn to leave.

And then there's Paul. Living out my fantasies in private was one thing. The seismic shift that happened when our bodies were knotted together, him whispering into my ear, was another thing entirely. Before, my flights of fancy had never collided with reality. Before, my skin had never known what it was like to touch his. Before, I'd never known that little bite I still feel on my shoulder.

Back to everyday life with all its ordinary gestures: sleeping with my body pressed up against Marine's, stroking those voluptuous curves I still love, the taste of apple pie taking me back to my childhood. Without the choking sensation in my throat. In the early morning, I go to meet Pascale on the boat that will soon be mine. I'm running from Marine, guiltily procrastinating, cheering myself up on the 1980s Bayliner I'm already so proud of. I follow Pascale's instructions and we laugh at how clumsy I am. We glide along in good spirits. The lake is more reassuring than the sea, its shoreline within eyeshot in every direction. She stops the engine, and we plunge blissfully into the sleepy morning water.

I'd decided over the course of the last three weeks that I would not, under any circumstances, become anyone's mistress. The unsuccessful candidate, frantically penetrated and doted on for the time it takes to consummate the act, then casually abandoned on the questionable sheets of an Ibis hotel on the outskirts of an industrial area. The weeping woman, clinging to her lover's neck when he goes to leave. The thirsty, hysterical supplicant, falling to her knees eagerly behind a door or hastily bent over the office desk on her stomach. I knew I couldn't do it. And I knew we wouldn't leave our respective partners. But that's all I knew. I had my doubts, too. Why, in that spontaneous, blissful moment, had I been able to focus solely on love and feelings? Perhaps it had simply been a question of alchemy and pheromones. I once read an article in a newspaper that said science could provide a pragmatic explanation for attraction. Was I even more stupid than those airheads with their vapid little love stories, who I'd looked down on at secondary school? Then there was the guilt, a constant that had tormented me from the cradle. It would rear its ugly head whenever Marine shot me a mischievous or affectionate glance, whenever she planted a wet kiss on my cheek and said: 'I love you.' I was waltzing along on an emotional roller-coaster mapped out according to my surges of desire and the agony of bereavement.

*

At work, I carry on as normal. I ignore the faint shiver that runs down between his shoulder blades when I shout a haughty, false-sounding 'Hello' to nobody in particular on the day of my return. I dive head first into my desk, piled high with files, and the sea of people offering their help. I listen and nod along to each person's compassionate expressions of sympathy. I submerge myself in mail and don't let myself go anywhere near his corridor. I turn everything off without so much as glancing over at his desk.

Then one day, as I'm staring into the chemical froth of the coffee from the office machine, I sense his presence before I see him. He closes the door and leans against the kitchen counter. With his index finger, he tucks a lock of my hair behind my ear. He gently presses his lips to the corner of my eyebrow, takes a deep breath, then turns to leave.

With him, it's all secrecy. With him, it's all silence and duplicity. I don't know how to deal with hypocrisy. My animal instinct takes over. Time to run. From both of them.

I invite myself to spend those autumnal weekends at Delphine's cabin. We've known each other five years now. Our origins brought us together, the mysteries of friendship took care of the rest, defying our fifteen-year age gap and polar-opposite personalities. I know she can help me make sense of my vile, rebellious behaviour with her sage, poetic reflections and wisdom. She was the one who introduced me to the *bisses*, narrow and easily walkable paths once constructed to irrigate plantations, wrapped horizontally around the steep mountains and hillsides. Absolute bliss. That autumn, after her knee operation, we trade in our more intrepid routes for strolls around Vercorin, a humble village with nothing but a church, a few cafes and a grocery store. There are still a few *mayens* here, log cabins set atop four stone stilts, beneath which inhabitants of our parents' generation used to store and dry their hay. We learned these little factoids about local architecture and the Valaisian microclimate in primary school from teachers who knew a thing or two about our heritage and were proud of it. But the Val d'Anniviers always seemed far away from home, as it was on the other side of the river Rhône. We didn't care about it back then, especially not me; I just wanted to go, go, go. The other side of the river wasn't far enough. Today, these houses, whether in their original state or meticulously renovated, seem exotic and fascinating even to a Valaisian like me. I had never had anyone to tuck me in at night and tell me stories about the olden days, nostalgic stories that embellish the harsh reality of mountain life. Delphine, on the other hand, spent her summers with her grandmother, who would tell her all kinds of tales, which she happily passes on to me. Now I no longer live there, now I've disowned my family and my past, I can finally reinvent my origins and maybe even come to cherish the ties I've aggressively been trying to cut myself free of.

Just three hours from Lausanne station, I arrive in a different country. First the train, then the bus that takes me to the cable car connecting the plains to Vercorin via a steep ascent over craggy rocks. This refuge clears my mind and helps my heart focus on the essential. We take the Tour du Mont route, wandering at a leisurely pace for a good hour. If we talk, it's only to make a comment about the vegetation, or to gasp in surprise when we turn a corner and stumble upon an intrepid chamois, native to the region, rustling about in the branches. We stop at a bench between the Swiss pines, and our gazes plunge down into the valley. That's all. There's nothing else. I have everything I need here.

In the morning, we light the fire in the wood burner and keep it going throughout the day. All the bed linen and crockery here once belonged to her grandmother. I appreciate them all the more because they're imprinted with the memories she's shared with me. In the evenings, I sit down with her family to eat fondue, pick at bits of dried meat and rye bread over a glass of wine or eat pasta smothered in cheese. Her grown-up children drop by, and we all play cards together, laughing and discussing light, trivial subjects. One Saturday evening, we sit outside beneath the larch trees on the rickety wooden benches around the fireplace built by her father. Her husband takes half a wheel of cheese to make raclette and we all wait patiently to be served. As he cooks, we talk or listen to the fire crackling, wrapped up in blankets. Raclette is a dish typical of our region, yet this is the first time I've ever eaten it. It's too convivial for a lonely, isolated family like mine. It's a humble dish made for sharing. As I console myself, I realize that what my parents didn't give me was an identity. Instead, I created one for myself based on festering hatred. These simple days temper the grievances buried deep within me and reconcile me with the sense of absence.

As the train rolls across the plain one day in late October, my stomach is still pleasantly numb from the brisolée – chestnuts roasted on the open fire, cheese and rye bread – and the grape must a local wine producer gave us in an old lemonade bottle. I'm glumly rereading a novel, my bare feet up on the chair in front of me. All of a sudden, he's there. Paul is there. Standing by my right thigh (I always choose a seat in the front row on the left-hand side so I can admire the lake, the one constant punctuating every stage of my new life). I sit up in my seat in surprise; he's already taking the seat opposite. He places a hand on my ankle to stop my nervous fidgeting. He smiles.

'What are you doing here?'

'Taking the train.'

I reach out and tenderly touch his cheek. He closes his eyes as I gently stroke them with my thumb. He kisses my palm. 'This is not a good idea, Paul. You know we can't do this.'

'No, I don't know. I miss you too much.'

'No.' I repeat the word as he shuffles forward in his seat, pressing his forehead against mine. 'No, no, no. I don't want secrecy and I don't want to leave Marine. There's no other solution. We have to end this.'

'We'll find a solution. There must be one. There always is.'

'No there isn't. Someone is bound to get hurt. I'm telling you there's no solution.'

I refrain from kissing him. The ticket inspector coughs; we show him our tickets. We remain silent for the rest of the trip, gazing out of the window, his hand resting on my ankle. He changes carriages just before Lausanne. I accidentally leave my copy of *Twenty-Four Hours in the Life of a Woman* on the train.

19

The mouth-watering smell of pumpkin soup fills the room. My customary hello, Marine's identical echo over the racket of the mixer. The phone rings. I find it on the living room coffee table. 'Hello?'

'Hi. It's Dad.'

Dad. As if it were the most natural thing in the world to say 'Dad'. A word he'd never once used in his life. And he certainly hadn't called me before. I grind my molars together.

'All Saints' Day is coming up. Are you coming to the cemetery?'

'...'

The sound of the mixer in the background stops. His hoarse, alcoholic's voice. 'Jeanne...'

'...'

'Jeanne, I'm sorry. I loved her. I'm so miserable now she's gone.'

Anger. Immense anger. Rumbling, rising. 'How dare you?' The volume increases with each sentence. 'How dare you?

Have you forgotten the time you threw Mum on the kitchen floor, sat on her chest, trapped her legs and hit her? Have you forgotten the time you dunked her head in the bathtub, like when you drowned Emma's cat? Have you forgotten the time you smashed my sister's face into a bowl of hot mashed potatoes just for talking and you didn't stop until the potatoes were as red as her face? Have you forgotten the time Mum dropped a bag of rice on the floor and you forced her to pick up the grains in her mouth, one by one? Have you forgotten all of that? Because I haven't. I have it playing on loop on my head. And Emma? Emma? EMMA? Do you remember? How you raped her? Do you remember? Do you remember, you bastard?'

There's sniffing and sobbing on the other end of the line. 'That's just the way it was back then.'

'What? What the fuck? What do you mean the way it was? What is wrong with you? It was like that because of you, you piece of shit. It wasn't like that, not for anyone else I know. I wasn't born in the Middle Ages, for fuck's sake! So take your whining elsewhere. I don't want to hear it. Drop dead. And be quick about it,' I screamed, my voice unrecognizable, terrible.

Drop dead. Marine was standing there, wide-eyed, petrified. This was a side of me she didn't know, details from my childhood I'd never told her. How many memories were there, eating me alive, rising from my guts without warning in the form of acid, keeping me awake all those hopeless, sleepless nights? I couldn't eat a thing after that.

I slept pressed up against her back, my hands balled into tight fists, tucked under my chin.

*

We cover the boat for winter. The pain and apathy set in once more. I don't have the strength to study for my boat licence. I fall into a despair that lasts for weeks. I go running early in the morning, the damp Lausanne winter penetrating my bones. I don't swim any more. I'm barely sleeping, losing weight. My brain is foggy, my mind slow. It's like having an eternal hangover. The daily routine, pragmatic, metronomic. Marine, running, work, Paul, our stolen meetings. He looks awful too. Then I don't hear anything for a few days.

'Paul?' (On the phone.)

'Yes?' (His weary reply.)

'What's going on?'

It all comes out. His wife's doubts. His uncharacteristic coldness and dour mood roused her suspicions. He denied it at first, then resolved to tell her the truth: he didn't love her any more. Carnage ensued – 'You have no idea.' The in-laws got involved. Questions were raised about his job. Obviously. She cried, made threats, used their daughter to blackmail him. An absolute mess. 'I need to let things settle. You were right. There is no solution. Not yet at least. I need some space. It's all too complicated.'

The city is in its best garb, glittering with white and gold lights. Marine insists we take a stroll through the streets, decked out in all their splendour for last-minute Christmas shoppers. 'Come on, let's get in the spirit and have some mulled wine!' She loves the Christmas season. She never tires of it as the years go by. She makes candied oranges, buttered caramels, rich coconut fondants, aniseed cookies, bricelets flavoured with lemon zest. She cooks up a meat pâté and the whole house is fragrant with spices. She lights candles every night, hangs a little star in the corner, places angels on the messy bookcase. One day she even arrives with a huge straw deer. Everything is cheerful, childlike. I go along with it. I would be stupid to let this woman go. She's what keeps me going. Some evenings she encourages me to talk, gently pushing me to dig for happy memories of things I did with Mum and Emma. There must be some. I can't think of any. It makes me cry. 'Let it all out. You'll feel better.' What am I doing, wallowing in this hellish affair with Paul?

January, with its endless oaths, is well under way. Gone is the hope that comes with the end-of-year festivities; the promise of spring is yet to arrive. I hate these short, windy, misty, grey days. There's not even snow, not like in my childhood. One Sunday morning, after a tiring jog, I do a few stretches in the car park in Vidy. I'm standing there like a flamingo, looking ridiculous, when I spot the silhouette of someone I recognize. The frame, lanky and rakish even with hunched shoulders, the hat, the English raincoat, hands in pockets. I'm still standing there on one leg as he makes his way over. I glare at him, chin tensing.

'I called in at your house. A woman there told me where to find you.'

What could the Doctor possibly want?

'I need to talk to you.'

'Can't it wait? I'm freezing.'

'No, I want to talk to you now. I have to leave at midday.'

Midday is three whole hours away. There's something about his tone, his status or perhaps his calm presence that demands deference. He exudes a kind of non-aggressive authority that doesn't allow for negotiation. I invite him to mine; I need to change. I don't negotiate, either.

Marine is good at dealing with the unexpected. By the time I've showered and thrown on jeans and a woollen jumper, he's sat there, at ease on the sofa, which is covered in a bohemian-looking fabric Marine found at a market. There's tea, coffee, biscuits and some sweet pastries she seems to have impressed him with. I sit facing him, cross-legged with my back straight, on a large red cushion. Marine makes herself scarce.

'All right,' he says, half-heartedly.

I notice he hasn't aged well.

'Since your mother died, I haven't stopped reflecting on things. For a long time, I wasn't sure whether I should come and apologize to you.

'What for? For being a coward?'

He nods, eyes full of tears. Thirty years have passed. I can understand why he's ashamed. I feel a twinge of empathy for this distinguished man. He's getting old now. I think back to that awful night, the trust I placed in him, the 'dear friend' that earned me my father's wrath irremediably. It's taken over my entire existence for long enough now that I'm ready to hear what he has to say.

'I knew. Not everything, but I knew. Everybody knew about your father. Nobody did anything. That's just the way it was. Nobody spoke up, nobody interfered with anybody else's lives. We all kept quiet. But as a doctor, I had a responsibility. I should have helped you. Back then, we didn't have the means we do today. But I should have, I could have found a solution. And you know… I was very fond of your mother.'

20

In his own modest way, he's as frank as he can be. They'd known each other all their lives. They loved each other the way children do. Innocently. During their adolescence, there were kisses behind barns, promises made. Then came the studies, the distance. It was as though she evaporated from his life. He started meeting others, women, one in particular. They moved back to the village where he was born, a village which, luckily for him, did not have a doctor at the time. He'd always harboured the childhood dream of becoming the village doctor.

'The next time I saw your mother, she was pregnant with you. I heard what she was going through. Not from her, from the village gossips. All you had to do was ask and tongues would start wagging. And I...' He takes a deep sigh. 'I had feelings for her. I wouldn't call it love. More a deep friendship.' Reminiscences of childhood, youth, her kindness, her timid nature. 'I was touched by her. I'd married an ambitious woman from a good family, and we'd had two children.

Every time I saw your mother, I was filled with sadness. It wasn't pity. But I did nothing, I was a hypocrite, I failed in my duty as a friend and as a doctor. I'm old now, but my lack of courage still eats away at me. More and more each day.

'If I'd done something… If only I'd done something. I should have persuaded her to leave. I should have helped you and her, found you a small apartment or a place in the city. And the rest… well, you know the rest. You remember that night. She hadn't explained anything when she called me to come and check you over. She didn't say anything once I arrived, either. But you did. And I buried my head in the sand. I was a coward, as you pointed out. I had applied for a job at the hospital shortly before. It was a good opportunity. My wife insisted on leaving Valais. She wanted more. She hated living there. Couldn't get used to the simple life.

'By all appearances, I've had a good life, as we say back home. But I've never forgotten your mother, or how I failed you. I paid for you to go to boarding school in Sion. That's the only thing she asked. She desperately wanted to save you from that place. She wanted to give you a chance. She made arrangements with my cousin, who became your teacher there, to make sure your father didn't find out. He thought everything was paid for by the state. They managed to keep the secret. I'd behaved appallingly. It was the least I could do.'

The sobs and convulsions take over, and there's nothing I can do about it. He, too, is sniffling. I weep for my mother's infinite love, for everything she did for me without saying a thing. How desperate she was to save me. I weep because of the ingratitude I showed her up until the end of her life, because of my own cowardice, my own selfishness. I tell him about the tiger, the 'dear friend', the admiration I once had for him.

He's sorry. More than sorry. He's mortified. He feels he's the one to blame. There's no denying it. We both are. I thank him for the school. He shakes his head. It's nothing. The least he could do.

'Does your wife know about the school fees?'

'No. I never told anyone.'

'I have one more question. Why are you telling me this now?'

He thinks for a long time, looking down at the floor. 'My whole life is a masquerade. At my age, you begin to take stock of things. And now my arrogance is sufficiently frayed, fortunately… I live a comfortable but hollow life. I've been lucky. Yet I'm full of sorrow. A sorrow that can't be cured' – that's the word he uses, *cured* – 'by work, friends, activities… I seek out distractions, temporary diversions from my melancholy. I've tried to forget you, to pretend… but I can't. My children have been spoiled rotten, but all they do is blame me. My wife lives her life and I just go along with it. You know as well as I do. I'm a coward through and through. I wanted to live in the village, to be a good doctor.' He sighs. 'I'm withering away in my sorrow, and I'll take it to the grave. I'm a bitter old man. Don't think I'm trying to redeem myself by coming to talk to you. I can't make amends for my cowardice. I've been volunteering with an association for years, helping people. It makes me feel better, makes people think I'm a good person. But I left you in your father's hands and disappeared. I can't make up for that. I simply wanted you to know that I knew, and that everything you think about me is true. I'm a coward and a despicable wretch. I can see you're doing well. But at what cost? Your mother and sister would still be alive had I intervened.'

Irrevocably bound by his confessions, we take one final look at one another, eyes misted over with sorrow.

'I have so many regrets,' he says finally, and I watch his elegant figure slip through the doorway.

For days, I racked my brains for childhood memories of Dr Fauchère. I looked for signs of his relationship with my mother from the times we'd met him, on the rare occasions I went into his practice. Had I ever picked up on compassionate gestures, signs of his affection for her? Or had he simply wanted to absolve himself of guilt?

A memory came to mind. At Emma's wake, I'd escaped to get some fresh air outside the limewashed walls of the tiny village chapel. When I went back inside, once the gawkers with their false sympathy and their Hail Marys had dispersed, I saw him walking up the little aisle. When he passed my mother, dignified and stiff with grief, he squeezed her shoulder. It was a tender gesture, natural in the circumstances, but considering what I now knew, I took it as a sign. She instinctively responded by tilting her cheek against the back of his hand. She didn't startle. It was a furtive gesture to acknowledge their friendly alliance.

I wanted to understand my mother's life and her choices. Did she have any regrets? What were her secrets? 'I have my dreams,' she'd once said to me. He hadn't been the only one who lacked courage. She had too. Why? And why had I judged her for it?

Who did I think I was to label others? Betraying Marine, is that what I called bravery? Who was I to judge? Like father, like daughter.

21

Coincidences happen when you're least expecting them. A few days after Dr Fauchère's visit, my father's only sister informed me that my father had been hospitalized. We no longer spoke, she and I, and I'd avoided her at both funerals. I must have been around ten years old the last time she'd come to visit. She'd walked into the kitchen while my father was brutally shaking my mother. We hadn't heard the doorbell ring over his crude insults. She materialized out of nowhere. 'Louis!' she screamed. Loud and clear. 'What?' he grunted in reply. That was it. She never came back again. She avoided us, like everyone else. If nobody saw the abuse, if nobody looked, then it didn't exist. The Doctor wasn't the only coward in the village.

My father had fainted in front of the house. The neighbours called an ambulance. Without elaborating much, my aunt told me he wasn't eating. He was letting himself die. 'It would be good if you came.'

He can die in a hole for all I care, I thought.

'I've hidden the house keys under a rock next to the doormat.'

I have the house all to myself. To rummage. To look for something that might help me understand my mother's choices. And perhaps even my own.

Without my mother's meticulous attention, the garden seems to have lost all its life. Even the rosemary bush is withering away against the wall. The walnut tree is looking glum, the rickety old fence has finally given up the ghost and is lying on the ground, which has been hardened by the cold. The frost-blackened flowers are drooping beneath clumps of frozen snow like little arms without bones. The whole garden screams of my father's laziness, carelessness and negligence. Inside, he's managed to strip away all the shine my mother worked hard to bring to the place by polishing it up as best she could.

The stench hits as soon as the door opens. I air the rooms out despite the February chill. Without thinking, I pile the empty bottles into bags, wash the mountain of dishes, throw his clothes into a corner of the room, root around for cleaning products. I blitz the place to get rid of the encrusted dirt and the smell. I want the house clean before I start rummaging. After five hours of scrubbing the bathroom and scouring the dirt clinging to the bottom of the toilet bowl, I call Marine. I am disgusted and disheartened by the level of degradation.

Her schedule as a social worker means she has the day off tomorrow. She arrives at seven in the evening and cooks pasta. The kitchen floor is so sticky, I can hear our trainers peeling away from the floor with each step. We open a bottle of cheap wine we find in the cellar next to the cheese. It's so old it tastes like soap. We drag my parents' mattress onto the floor in the living room. Marine falls into a deep sleep. The morning light keeps me awake.

Had I stopped to think, I wouldn't have gone into Paul's office. We'd been carefully avoiding each other, having made the decision to remain with our respective partners and put an end to our adulterous tryst. By all appearances, we'd become the living dead, but we stood firm. Our eyes locked each time we spotted each other from a distance. With each fleeting but unmistakable glance, we confessed to one another that we hadn't given up hope.

Marine and I clean up the place efficiently. In the courtyard, we make a pile of things to throw away. I revisit my old room and Emma's. The furniture is old and dusty but still intact.

There's nothing lying around. Nothing in the drawers. Nothing in the wardrobes but linen, a few old things and one or two items of threadbare clothing. I come across a scarf I'd given to Mum as a gift, balled up and torn.

Once the floor is as shiny as possible, we sit down, exhausted, on a little bench we've moved under the bare walnut tree.

That's when I see it. The storeroom window. I bolt back inside like a woman possessed and run up the steps round the back of the house. Beneath the roof, among the wooden beams, cobwebs and daylight streaming in between the tiles, I'm certain I've found a hiding place.

The space, which my father never entered, is surprisingly neat and tidy. Boxes. Two dozen or so. Inside, there are books. I open them one by one. Books. Nothing else. No letters, no diary. Nothing. Just books. I fall to the floor like a puppet, legs spread, arms dangling by my sides, head empty. Fuck it! I kick one of the piles and thrash at the books at though struck by the dancing plague. All my books from childhood and adolescence, an old dictionary and a Bible. All these memories, jumbled up together. I feel nothing.

I think about Paul, the traces our connection would leave behind. There are none. They're there under my skin, there's no evidence. All my secrets, my anger, my thoughts, only exist inside of me. Nobody would ever be able to find a thing. What the hell am I even looking for? Standing there helplessly beneath the roof, in the light streaming through the cracks in the wind- and snow-weathered tiles, I spot an old-fashioned, round key on the floor. It must have slipped out of its hiding place in one of the books.

'Marine!' I call out, rushing towards her. 'I've found it, I've found it.' She tells me not to get too excited. It might be nothing. 'Are you kidding? Hidden in a book in a pile of boxes? I can't believe it!' She concedes. We check the rooms methodically, one by one. Nothing.

'Think! Somewhere she knew your father would never find it, somewhere he never goes.'

I race downstairs to the utility room. It's spartan, damp concrete from floor to ceiling, a rectangular sink and shelves hidden behind a floral curtain. A plastic crate, tongs, brand-new bars of Marseille soap. Stain removal sprays, washing powder in cardboard boxes. That's it. I open them up. The first is almost full. The second is empty. Inside the third, a rectangular box, resting on its side. Mum has left me her secrets. Not as a confession. But for me. How many times did she tell me to stop asking questions?

Dr Fauchère's name is Simon. There's a mix of post-cards he and I sent over the years. Tourist snapshots of Madrid, Paris and Berlin, reproductions of classical paintings. *Thoughts*, S. Never anything more. Their discreet way of avoiding the prying eyes of the postman and my father. They all date from after he left the village. That same signature, scribbled from the United States, European capitals, Lausanne. At the bottom of the box, a slim notebook, yellowed and gnawed at by the years, filled with extracts of poems she copied out.

> In my sorrow, nothing moves
> Wait as I might, no one comes
> Not in the day, not in the night,
> Nothing remains of what I once was.
> *Emma – 1989*

I recognize Paul Éluard's verses but had no idea she knew them too. Probably another of her bookshop discoveries. Another page covered in my mother's cursive: verses of 'Tomorrow at Dawn' by Victor Hugo one after the other, with no line breaks. In the top right-hand corner: 1993.

Emma, all this time. The grief of a mother who has lost a child. Another thing we mustn't talk about.

Another letter, dated one month before she died:

My dearest Claire,

I was pleased to see you again at my cousin's funeral. I only regret that we did not have the opportunity to talk. May I call you to arrange to meet again?

Simon

I can't begin to explain the terrible sadness I felt. The sense of waste. She had suffered in silence. Emma's death had seized her heart while mine turned to stone. Rotten to the core. Like him. And a coward, like the Doctor.

Too late for regrets, excuses, forgiveness. She's dead now.

22

They tell me my father's condition is deteriorating. I stubbornly refuse to go to his bedside. Two days later, after the wooden box, they tell me it's now or never.

I have to see him again. Marine comes with me; I can't be alone with him. He's lying down. Repulsive. A pungent smell fills the room, his breath, his urine or the stench of panic being released from his dying body. I don't know. A wave of nausea hits me. He looks miserable. I should feel sorry for him, a twinge of empathy at least. Nothing, I feel nothing. Not even pity. The nurse tells me that if we put him in a wheelchair, we can take him for a walk. Marine pushes him. I'm not even capable of doing that. I trail behind them. He speaks slowly, tripping over his words. Just lifting the coffee cup to his lips takes an eternity. I look away, irritated. No sooner has it passed his lips than the brown liquid brims over and dribbles down his chin. He looks at Marine, sheepish and distraught, and says in a trembling voice: 'I can feel it running down my face, but I don't know how to drink any more.' Gently, she wipes the coffee away with a paper towel. He's disgusting. I don't feel an ounce of affection for him and I'm not ashamed. His whining continues: 'I miss Claire.' I get up from the table and busy myself by the buffet in the 1980s cafeteria. It hasn't changed since it was built, identical down to the furniture. We used to call it 'the new hospital'. When Emma had an appendectomy, Mum and I would come to visit her. We sat right here, in the same spot, at the round table. She was full of beans even then. Hospitals mean visitors and presents. Perhaps a little doll or a stuffed toy. Her present was a tube of cream. She would lend it to me, sparingly. The tube had to last as long as possible; it would never be replaced. I can still remember the smell.

Back in the bedroom, Marine puts him in a chair next to the window so he can look at the chestnut trees in the park, the apple trees scattered across the Rhône valley, gently shaking off the winter. I call the nurse to come and help us. At no point do I touch him.

Finally, it's time to go. Marine bends over to kiss his cheek. I stand there at his swollen feet. He's looking at me with a terrible sadness in his eyes. He knows this is it now. If his beliefs are anything to go by, hell will be waiting for him on the other side. Or maybe the years of repenting like a hangdog, his declarations of love for my mother, were all to cleanse him of his sins. Smart man. God forgives. But not me. 'Bye then,' I say.

He grabs my wrist, his eyes imploring me. 'Please! Don't.' He's about to start bawling. He's struggling to speak. I'm exasperated before the inevitable litany even begins. 'I know you hate me. But I love you.' He pauses before adding: 'I'm sorry.'

Marine is weeping softly behind me, choking back sobs. If this were a film, it would be enough to make anyone cry. But I'm not anyone. I'm the daughter of this monster. I'm the woman who cheats, I'm the woman who hits, I'm the woman made of stone, I'm the woman who's rotten to the core, I'm the daughter who didn't save her mother or her sister, I'm the daughter of a murderer, I'm the hollow woman, I'm the daughter watching her father die, I'm the woman who ignores her girlfriend's pleas: 'Make peace.'

I'm the woman who can't forgive.

I look at him – not at him, but through him. I feel a little stab of emotion, of fear, in my belly. I look at him again.

Then I spit in his face.

In the fraction of a second it takes for the fluid to hit him, I want to rewind the tape. Erase the bubbles of saliva between his eyes. I should have rushed to his feet, put my head in his lap, said that fucking word: 'Sorry.'

Nothing will ever be the same after this. Nothing can ever be innocent again. Every time Marine looks at me, she'll see that trickle of slime. That filthy gesture has stripped away what was left of my humanity.

If only I'd known. If only I'd known. Maybe, deep down, I did. I knew subconsciously that this terrible, humiliating, demeaning gesture, both for him and for me worse than a slap or an insult, worse than my arrogance, worse than my pride, would have its consequences. I knew I would never be able to erase it. Not from Marine's memory. Not from mine.

He died in the early hours of the morning. In the half-light before daybreak.

23

The death of my father did nothing to liberate me. If anything, it weighed on me even more than the deaths of my mother and sister. I felt no sorrow. The absence of sadness was not a fantasy in which I'd enveloped myself to keep others at a distance, nor a survival mechanism. I genuinely felt no pain. I would have preferred a lump in my throat to a knot in my stomach. The hatred and anger had solidified. I was rotting away. I hated what I was becoming. Unable to forgive, unable to cast off the stinking rags of my childhood. The more I hated myself, the more I shut myself away. Marine no longer tried to get me to talk. Though the kindness she showed me was genuine, that was simply who she was. My spit had driven a wedge between us. It had exceeded even the limits of her extraordinary tolerance.

There was hardly anything we couldn't resolve between us. Had I shown any remorse, she would have found it in her heart to wipe the slate clean. Instead, I punished myself by standing firm in my own impenetrable anger. I could have backtracked. I found myself incapable.

I could have kept the ugly truth from Paul. Instead, in a restaurant one evening, shortly after my father's death, I blurted it out: 'The night before my father died, he asked my forgiveness. I spat in his face.' I said the words deliberately. That vile gesture replayed in my mind. It was my way of pushing Paul away. I wanted him to give up on me. It's what I deserved. I sat there, arms crossed, torso stiff, defiant. His breath caught in his chest. Just for a second, as he took it in. He stroked my arm. I tried to be sarcastic and self-assured, I wanted to show him I had no regrets. But telling him the story only proved the opposite.

'What do you want, Jeanne? Do you want me to hate you? There's only one person here who hates you, and it isn't me.'

I knew then that he truly loved me. He knew better than I did that this version of me was nothing more than an expression of pain. My eyes welled up. He paid; we went out into the chill night air. When we got to the street corner, he stopped and wrapped his arms around me. He rocked me gently, his lips pressed to my forehead. I was overwhelmed by the tenderness swelling up in my chest. In tears, I threw my arms around him and held him tight in desperation. It was simple and intense. I couldn't tear off the layers of pain clinging to me like brambles. The anger had crept its way under my skin. Nothing could calm the waves roaring inside me. Nothing except moments like these with him. I was walking a tightrope, and all I had to do was jump off on the right side. It wouldn't have taken much. All I had to do was make the choice to stop the worms from eating me alive, day after day. He held my face in his hands and looked me in the eye. The knowledge that I couldn't find peace was causing him pain and distress. But his kindness and sincerity were finding their way in. The connection we had could not be severed, despite my dreadful way of relating to the world.

'I left my wife.'

I left my wife. That was it. No questions, no dressing it up, no discussions about the implications for him.

I left my wife. He was free. And he wasn't asking anything of me. We went to a hotel.

It wouldn't have taken much.

When I came home on the Saturday, Marine was making coffee, her face drained of its characteristic warmth. It was late in the morning. I hadn't anticipated spending the night with Paul. No hello. I was shamefaced, yet I didn't feel guilty any more. 'Paul,' she said.

She looked at me with her big green eyes, her face streaked with tears from the night before. I had to tell the truth, out of respect for her. I nodded and sat down. I braced myself for a scene, reproaches, an argument. Head down, shoulders up, like a boxer parrying blows.

'I don't want the details. Please. I had an inkling the first time we met at the bistro. It was the way he smiled at you. But I didn't think any more of it. Then, at your mum's funeral, I knew. I know you. You're always true to yourself. So what do you want to do now?'

'I don't know.'

'I don't like the person you're becoming. You're not the only one who's suffered. You're not the only one who had a difficult childhood. But the way you treat us, all of us. Me, Paul, I imagine, your friends, our friends… You didn't have it in you to make peace with an old man who asked for your forgiveness. He may have been a bastard, the worst of the worst, but you spat in his face, Jeanne. You're wallowing in the mire, perpetuating the suffering. There's nothing more I can do for you. I loved you so much. I still do. But I'm tired, Jeanne. I'm tired.'

I threw a few things in an old duffel bag. Marine stayed at the kitchen table, rooted to the spot. 'I'm sorry. I'm going to Valais for a few days.' I went to move towards her, but the look in her eye stopped me.

'OK. We'll talk when you get back.'

My instinct told me to throw my arms around her. I ignored it and fled.

Mechanically, I took the train to Valais, the keys to my childhood home in my jacket pocket. A notary had contacted me after my father's death. I was an orphaned heiress. The house, two fields in a forest a little north of our commune, a few thousand francs in a bank account (Mum never had any money because he hoarded it all), and no debt, I was told. The lawyer bored me with his tedious words. I put on a brave face. I had to – the drab office and all the jargon made the place and the situation seem more serious than it needed to be. Once the incomprehensible lecture was over, I asked to draw up a will for myself. Just a few official documents to sign. Marine would get everything. I didn't have to think twice about it. If nothing else, she could sell the lot and keep the money as a nest egg. Paul would get the boat; he knew how to sail.

Once the lake is out of sight, once I can no longer gaze at the shimmer of the sun on the water, once the fisherman I glimpse through the window, perched on a grey rock, disappears from view, I call Delphine. For so long, I was unable to understand Valaisians and their visceral need always to return home. To me, it was a form of punishment. I was scornful of their childish, naive attachment to their canton, but deep down I envied them. The sweetness of returning to one's roots. Now I was alone, my instinct was to return home too.

The peonies are uncrumpling their petals, the grass is covered in a carpet of campanula; anemones and giant poppies in dusty pinks and flaming reds have taken over the garden. Delphine and I open all the windows to let the scent of spring inside. We make coffee and talk about her children and the chalet. They're spending more time there these days. She can sense I'm not well, but she's too prudent, too modest to pry. It's only when the sun goes down and the wine starts flowing that I'm able to find the words to wash away the heaviness in my stomach. I talk about Paul. I talk about my deep affection for Marine. I talk about my father, that unforgivable gesture. I talk about my mother's box, Dr Fauchère. I talk the way they talk in confession. I let it all out, all the things clogging me up from the inside. 'My heart has dried up,' I say.

She replies without missing a beat. 'You'll find your watering can.'

We laugh at the naive sentiment, but there's an eloquence to it. I know what I ought to do. Start seeing a therapist again, Bernard or someone else. Quit my job. Distance myself from Paul and Marine to get some clarity. Live in this house to give myself a chance to recharge, or in the chalet ('if it's too difficult for you to be here'). I know all this. But it's one thing knowing, having the means. It's another thing doing.

I would have given anything to be able to sustain myself with happy memories. To be able to look back with a joyful heart on the little ladybird sticker that made Mum's face light up, the squirrel Emma and I tried in vain to capture for an entire afternoon, Paul sleeping up against my back, my body immersed in the glittering water of Lake Geneva as the sky explodes into red, kisses on the forehead, watching a breathtaking sunset with Marine, a stranger saying thank you with a smile, the turquoise water of the lake in Moiry, the winding paths of the *bisses*, all the terraces, all the gatherings, the sound of Nina Simone's voice, reading *The Man Who Planted Trees* a thousand times over.

Instead, I remain in this limbo of chaos. A state of destructive restlessness. And I know I'll never tear myself away.

24

When morning comes, the moment the sun rises, I know. I know that of all the places I've visited, few have left their mark. Grains of sand, fine and beige or dark and coarse; narrow, dirty streets; glowing city lights; monuments, some glorious, others in ruins; exotic spices; paintings, some I admired, others I didn't understand. What remains of all these things? The churches I visited, though my heart wept for the absence of that Divine Love that had forsaken me; candles lit with a childish hope that was never enough to appease my anger. What becomes of all of that? Of my fifteen thousand days, how many have brought me hope for life? How many do I still remember?

Everything brings me back to the place I've been trying to escape. And yet I could turn the page, live without fear, stop startling at every noise, every phone call, every raised voice. He's not here any more. And yet he is. He's always here. And what of the thousands of pages I've read, the hundreds of songs I've heard? How much do I remember? So little. Now I know. I know I never found meaning. I never pretended. I lived from one day to the next, but not one of those days was able to erase the fear and rage I carry from my childhood. It's such a small thing, childhood. But for me, it's all there is. I don't know how to take refuge anywhere else.

I know nothing will ever move me enough to turn things around. Nothing can break down this anger. I know the foundations of my childhood aren't strong enough to support me. I think of how the villagers turn over the earth in their gardens each spring, how the village elders used to say: 'It doesn't matter how much fertilizer you add, nothing will ever grow.' The earth's no good. I'm no good. Nothing will ever grow. Bad soil, bad seed.

At eight in the morning, I call Paul. It's a Sunday in May. I love the month of May, how it stays for a while to punctuate the interminable nights. I love the hope it brings as it gently draws out the days. I love the scents that spring up among the blades of grass. I love how the earth becomes fertile, teeming with clusters of tulips, gentians, lily of the valley. I love the plump, majestic peonies as much as the storms that can destroy them in a matter of minutes. I love the sun's warmth, still tender. I love that I can pull on a cardigan in the evening and still sit outside.

Two hours later, his car pulls up beneath the walnut tree. The sight of him sends a shiver down my spine. It's as though I'm seeing him for the first time. I'm moved by the way he walks, his smile, his tender sincerity. I can't tell him that his love has only ever scratched the surface of my soul.

That night, I'm lying on my side, he on his back, one arm behind his head. I look but don't touch. Now I know he doesn't snore, he takes his coffee without sugar, he avoids shaving if he can, he wears boxer shorts and a white T-shirt under his shirt. I know the name of his childhood crush, that he never managed to finish *Ulysses*. I know he used to sleep in his brother's bed, that they put a dent in the family car twice after a few too many drinks. I know that his dreams are simple, that he doesn't know how to cut the cheese for raclette. I know that he spent his summers with his maternal grandmother, that he hates shellfish and Lars von Trier, that he loves gianduja and full-bodied wine. I know he's optimistic, confident and easy-going. I know he believes in us.

I also know we'll never experience the suffocating heat of Matera in July, never be woken up in the middle of the night by the children crying, never leave in the early hours and drive for miles before catching the first glimpse of the sea, never walk into the house, shaking the snow off our coats, never wander through the streets of Rome or Seville, never burst out laughing in the middle of an argument, never lounge around in our pyjamas or host big dinner parties under the apple trees. I know he'll never get on my nerves, and that I'll never yell at him for coming home late. I know we'll never experience the petty bickering that goes hand in hand with domestic life.

As an excuse to leave early the next day, I tell him I have to meet my aunt. We put off saying goodbye, idling beneath the walnut tree.

'You know we could find a way. I could live here and commute.'

'Yes, I suppose you could.'

I breathe in his familiar scent, trace the hollow between his collarbones with the tip of my index finger. He kisses me on the forehead. I place my hand on his chest to feel his heartbeat.

I put away the breakfast things.

The jam drips onto the table. I don't feel moved.

I get ready slowly, for the last time.

I put on my navy-blue skirt. The one with the pleats.

My favourite.

ACKNOWLEDGEMENTS

Thank you to

Eddy, for his unfailing support.

Robert Seethaler, for his inspired question.

Sabine, for her open arms.

Sophie, Carole, Juliette, Gaëlle, for their strong faith.

Anne and Phidias, for the lively exchanges.

Stéphane, for his impartial criticism.

GLOSSARY

bisse — An irrigation system typically found in the Valais region, used to transport water from Alpine streams to farmland areas. The *bisses* are still used to water vines today but have also become part of the region's heritage and are popular walking routes.

bricelet — A thin, buttery biscuit that requires patience and skill to prepare. Usually eaten at Christmas time.

brisolée — A Valaisian dish served in the autumn, consisting of roasted chestnuts, cheeses, dried meat, rye bread, grapes, apples and grape must.

coujenaze — A Valaisian dialect word that literally means 'cooking', coujenaze is a simple, vegetable-based, country-style dish. Recipes vary seasonally and between regions and families.

foehn — A dry, warm wind typical of the Valais region. In Swiss French, the word also means 'hairdryer'.

fondant — A type of confectionery typically eaten on New Year's Eve and made from a mixture of melted chocolate and coconut fat. The mixture is poured into little coloured paper moulds and left in the fridge to set.

Goron	Valaisian red wine, made from a blend of Pinot Noir and Gamay. A humble wine that's easy to drink, Goron is a good wine for all occasions, often served as an aperitif or used in cooking.
mayen	Rustic Alpine dwellings found in the Valais region.

Transforming a manuscript into the book you hold in your hands is a group project.

Sarah Jollien-Fardel and Holly James would like to thank everyone who helped to publish *My Favourite* in English:

THE INDIGO PRESS TEAM

Susie Nicklin
Phoebe Barker
Michelle O'Neill

JACKET DESIGN

Luke Bird

EDITORIAL PRODUCTION

Tetragon
Sarah Terry
Bryan Karetnyk

PRESS

Rebecca Gray

The Indigo Press is an independent publisher of contemporary fiction and non-fiction, based in London. Guided by a spirit of internationalism, feminism and social justice, we publish books to make readers see the world afresh, question their behaviour and beliefs, and imagine a better future.

Browse our books and sign up to our newsletter for special offers and discounts:

theindigopress.com

Follow *The Indigo Press* on social media for the latest news, events and more:

@PressIndigoThe
@TheIndigoPress
@TheIndigoPress
The Indigo Press
@theindigopress

MY FAVOURITE

by

SARAH JOLLIEN-FARDEL

Translated from the French by
HOLLY JAMES

In the 1970s, in a village high up in the Swiss Valais mountains, everyone knows everything and no one says anything. Jeanne learns from an early age to dodge her father's abuse, but her mother and sister resign themselves to his brutality. One day, when she is eight, he attacks her viciously, angered by her self-assurance. Convinced the village doctor will put an end to their nightmare, she is shocked by his silence.

From then on, Jeanne's hatred of her father and her disgust at the doctor's cowardice drive her on. At boarding school she experiences five years of respite, but is then triggered by an unbearable replica of the violence that started it all. Moving to Lausanne, unable to come to terms with her past and to engage fully with life, she nevertheless finds solace in the arms of lovers and in the waters of Lake Geneva, while further tragedy fuels her rage.

My Favourite is a powerful novel about departure and return, about love, guilt and shame, and the paralysing effects of trauma. Sarah Jollien-Fardel forcefully describes the price to be paid for Jeanne's hard-won emancipation, as history inexorably repeats itself.

© Marie Pierre Cravedi

SARAH JOLLIEN-FARDEL grew up in a village in the Hérens district of Valais, Switzerland. She lived in Lausanne for several years before moving back to her home canton with her husband and two sons. She trained as a journalist and has written for numerous local and national newspapers. *My Favourite*, a runaway bestseller published in French as *Sa préférée*, is her first novel.

HOLLY JAMES is a British literary translator based in Paris.

© Mary Rogers

ACCOLADES

Prix du Goncourt des détenus 2022
Choix Goncourt de la Suisse 2022
Prix du roman Fnac 2022
Prix de la librairie Millepages 2022 (Vincennes)
Shortlisted for the Prix Goncourt des Lycéens 2022
Longlisted for the Prix Audiolib 2023
Longlisted for the Prix du Barreau de Marseille 2023
Longlisted for the Festival du premier roman de Chambéry 2023
Longlisted for the Prix Goncourt 2022 (1st list)
Longlisted for the Prix des lecteurs de la Ville de Lausanne 2023
Longlisted for the Prix Envoyé par La Poste 2022

PRAISE FOR

My Favourite

'The novel grapples with questions about how society often closes their eyes to the brutality of domestic abuse and the marks it leaves on children. About what it means to become a young woman and build a life away from home penetrated by doubt of self-worth and inflicted guilt. A poignant story, narrated with finesse and boldness.'

NATALIYA DELEVA,
AUTHOR OF *FOUR MINUTES* AND *ARRIVAL*

'The strength of this debut novel … is due as much to the physical description of this middle-aged patriarchal dictator as to the manner in which Jeanne, "born dead", tells of her escape and survival.'

LE NOUVEL OBSERVATEUR, JÉRÔME GARCIN

'A violent man makes life hell for his wife and daughters. This book is a remarkable debut.'

LE MONDE DES LIVRES, DENIS COSNARD

'Thanks to its clipped diction, *My Favourite* is exceptional, moving and fierce, proud of its often elliptical style, reflecting its title.'

LIBÉRATION, VIRGINIE BLOCH-LAINÉ

'One can hardly believe that this is a debut, as its Swiss author, Sarah Jollien-Fardel, demonstrates her mastery and composure during the implacable outcome of events and human behaviour.'

L'EXPRESS, MARIANNE PAYOT

THE
INDIGO
PRESS